REFUGEE TALES

REFUGEE TALES

VOLUME II

Edited by
David Herd & Anna Pincus

ISBN 1910974307
ISBN-13 978-1910974308

Proceeds from this book go to the following two charities:
Gatwick Detainees Welfare Group and Kent Refugee Help.

The publisher gratefully acknowledges the support of Arts Council England.

Supported using public funding by

**ARTS COUNCIL
ENGLAND**

Contents

Prologue

Listen, friend
We hold this truth
To be self-evident
That a person
Who has a story
Requires space –
To start
We set this out
A simple requirement
In language
That in justice
As it is told
A person's story
Be accorded
Its place.

That's where we begin
Think of it as
A basic entitlement
Like walking
Telling stories
Occupying the landscape
In the heat of the sun –
Out of Canterbury
To reassert
The ancient covenant
That the State
As it is constituted

Shall not detain
Indefinitely.

It's where we start out
That people might
Simply circulate
Not stigmatised
For seeking asylum
In this straunge stronde
But listened to
As they tell their tales
That hearing we might shape
A polity –
Tender
Real
Comprehending welcome.

The Student's Tale

as told to

Helen Macdonald

THERE'S A WINDOW AND the rattle of a taxi and grapes on the table, black ones, sweet ones, and the taxi is also black and there's a woman inside it, a charity volunteer who befriended you when you were in detention, and she's leaning to pay the driver and through the dust and bloom of the glass I see you standing on the pavement next to the open taxi door and your back is turned towards me so all I can see are your shoulders hunched in a blue denim jacket. They're set in a line that speaks of concern. Not for yourself, but for the woman who is paying the fare. I wave through the window and you turn and see me and smile hello.

This is a borrowed house that we're talking in. It's not my home.

We sit at the table and I don't know where to begin.

I don't know anything about you.

It is hard to ask questions.

You want me to ask questions, because you say it is easier to answer questions than tell your story. I don't want to ask you questions, because I think of all the questions you must have been asked before. But you want me to ask you questions, and so I begin with: 'When did you get here?' And you write, in careful Persian numerals, *12, 2016.* December. And I ask more questions, and you answer them, and when the English words won't come, you translate using your phone, and this takes some time, and the sun slaps its flat gold light upon the table and the bowl of grapes and the teapot, all these quiet domestic things, as I wait to know what you might mean. Here are the words you look up while we talk: *Apostate. Bigoted. Depraved. Hide.*

You are a student of epidemiology. Epidemiologists study the mode of transmission of disease, the way it runs through populations from person to person. You tell me that back in your country you used to meet with your friends in your restaurant at night so you could talk of Christianity and read the Bible. There were Christian signs in your restaurant. You knew that you might be arrested for doing this. Secrecy is paramount. But faith is also faith.

This is what happens when you are denounced as an apostate. The authorities speak of you as if you were one of the agents of disease that you have studied. At prayers one Friday they denounce you by name in five regions, two cities and three villages.

They said that a woman at your university had depraved you, by which they meant she had encouraged you to become a Christian. They said that you had changed your religion. And that now you possess this faith, you spread it to other men.

They see your belief as a contagious disease. They want to isolate it, contain it, and like all such malevolent metaphors that equate morality with health, the cure is always extinguishment. You know what happens to apostates, to those who have changed their religion, in your country. Even I know what happens. I am holding my breath just thinking of it.

When the intelligence services came looking for you at your grandmother's home she called you and told you that these men were your friends even though they spoke the wrong language for the region and they were wearing distinctive clothes that made it obvious, really, who they were, and why they were there, but she was old and you couldn't blame her for expecting friendship when what was offered was its scorched obverse. Your uncle knew better. He told you to flee. 'Your life is in danger,' he said. Truth. So you fled. You left everything.

You drove from city to city and in a city more distant, met two friends of your uncle. They told you they could take you to Turkey with others by car. And once you were there, you wondered where you should go. Your uncle said, 'The UK is good,' and he offered to pay the smuggling agents to get you here. The car unloaded you all in an unkempt garden and you all had to hide there until the middle of the night when the truck came, and you got in.

Days in the darkness inside a lorry on its way north. A freezer truck. 'How many people were in there with you?' I ask. And you laugh, and say, 'Ten? I don't know... It was dark!' And I laugh too, a little ashamed, and wonder why I want to press you for these little details. None of us want to know what this is like. We don't want to know how it feels to not eat or drink or sleep for five days and nights, to be sustained in terror and darkness merely through the hope that there is light on the other side. None of us want to know what it feels like to be threatened with a knife, as you were threatened. To be held at gunpoint by people you have paid to bring you to safety.

You say, it was 'the worst feeling.' Then you say it again. 'The worst feeling.'

'Several times,' you tell me, 'I see my death.'

Then you say it again. 'I see my death.'

The hardest things, I realise, you are saying them all twice.

And what I am thinking, as you say 'sorry' into the silence while you wait to be able to once again speak, is this. I think of how scientists have only just found out how our brains make memories. They used to think that we record a short term memory, then archive it later, move it to a different part of the brain to store it long term. But now they've discovered that the brain always records two tracks at once. That it is always taping two stories in parallel. Short-term memories, long-term memories, two tracks of running recollection, memory doubled. Always doubled.

Which makes everything that ever happens to us happen twice.

Which makes us always beings split in two.

You are an epidemiologist. You are a refugee.

You are also an asylum seeker who has seen detention centre inmates cut themselves with razors, lash out in violence, numb themselves with spice.

The government wants to send you back to Greece, but that would be dangerous because of people there who know who you are, who have threatened you, who have contacts with the authorities back home. So now you are in a hostel, with four hundred others. You have to sign in once in the morning and once again at night. You are a student, a brother, a son, who manages to speak to your family back home through Telegram, through WhatsApp, and you are also a man who asks the receptionist for help when violence or sickness breaks out in the hostel and watches the receptionist shrug, dismissively, and no help comes. All the things you see between refugees, you tell me, 'are harmful for brain, for mind, for spirit.' You say, of the hostel, in the quietest, gentlest voice, that there, 'nothing is good, really. Nothing is good. It is a very nasty place.' You tell me, twice, that 'some people have not even any clothes.'

In December you'd called the police from the frozen dark inside the lorry. The police opened the doors and took you to a cell, questioned you, detained you for 72 hours. And when you requested asylum they moved you to an immigration detention centre. You were there for 80 days. I have heard a lot about the conditions there, this place that is known as a hellhole. So it is a mark of your kindly reticence that all you can say about it is, 'The situation in detention was very bad.'

You are a refugee who has taken deep breaths to sing songs in this detention centre where people are held indefinitely and you are also a man sitting at a sunny dining table laughing out loud at your mistake when you realise that you said your father is 'literature' when what you meant to say was your father is 'illiterate'. You are a man who can laugh at the ridiculousness of mistranslation, and you are also a man who has left a life behind, your father, your little brother, your ailing family members, and every corner of home, and that loss pours from you, silent through the laughter, like a cold current of air that sinks to the floor and fills the room beneath everything light that is spoken here.

You don't want to talk about yourself, except to give the facts. What you want to talk about are the problems facing the people around you. Your charity volunteer friend tells me that after you saw an advert for Water Aid you asked her to donate what little funds you had to the children who were suffering, because the way the system works, you weren't allowed to do it yourself. She tells me, though she apologises for speaking because it is not her story, that you have been buying fruit and lentils for the children in the hostel, because the food is so bad it makes people sick, and you can see the children are malnourished.

You are a man whose eyes are bright with unspilled tears when you tell me of the horror of your journey here. But when you think of the people who have shown you kindness? That is when you break down and cry. You say, of the woman sitting with us, 'I would maybe have suicide, without her.' When I ask you if the people in the city where you live are good to you, you say yes, because if you ask them an address, they will tell you where it is. They will tell you where it is.

I think about all the stories we tell of refugees and how they are always one story or another, never both at once. Tragic stories or threatening stories. Victims or aggressors. Never complicated, always simple, always with clean edges. Easy pigeonholes to fit people who have been forced to take wing.

But a hole is not just a pigeonhole. It's the space between two things. It's a hole that's the gap between a word in Urami or in Farsi and a word in English. It's the space between past and future, between old lives and new. Between years. When the new year came in March you went to the park in the city where the hostel is, and you sang songs welcoming the new year by the water of the lake. What can a new year mean, when you are young, and all you are able to do is wait.

'I want to be useful,' you say. 'I don't want to spend my time in the hostel, waiting.' And then you rub your eyes with one hand and you say, 'Please pray for me.' You say, 'This issue is very distracted my brain, my mind. I want to quickly take a part in this society. And the culture. At the moment I haven't any certificate, because I am an asylum seeker. And I don't take a part in helping people because I don't have any money, I don't have any device for helping the people, and I think my living is very precious. Precious?' You try the word out as a question, as if the word is itself somehow wrong.

'I don't like be spend it by the time, waiting,' you say. 'Because I am young.'

You are young. You are a student, an epidemiologist, a Christian, a refugee. You want to help people so much it hurts my heart. You are a man who I drive, after we have talked that afternoon, to the hospital so we can take a photograph of you standing outside the School for Clinical Medicine, because bound up in a sense of your future is this brightness, that you might one day be able to help, to work in medicine here. And you are also a man who tips back his head and laughs when we discover that the school has been closed for rebuilding, and the windows are boarded up and the palings mean we can't see the building at all. We take pictures anyway. Us in front of the barriers. You alone, you with your companion, you with me. We are all, all of us waiting while the world is rebuilt.

The Lover's Tale

as told to

Kamila Shamsie

JOHN'S CHILDHOOD AMBITION WAS to be a pilot. Let's sit with that a while. A boy grew up, like so many other boys all over the world, watching the skies, imagining himself in the endless blue. What do all these boys dream of? Of watching the world from above, of air starts and power-off glides, of aerial somersaults, of moonlit sorties, of racing through the clouds in 15,000 tonnes of machinery, of the attractiveness of being a man in uniform? Universal dreams, and not only boys dream them, of course. As universal as love, as family loyalty, as friendship, as kindness, as fear. And like love, loyalty, friendship, kindness and fear, the dream of being a pilot – however universal in its outlines – must exist and play itself out in very particular circumstances. In John's case, the circumstances start with place – the country of his birth and upbringing: _____. And _____ is where he started the story, when we met in London in a room made smaller than it needed to be by the excessive furniture – round table, too many chairs – crammed into it.

'I'm from _____,' he said. 'It's a small country. The government is a kind of a dictatorship. It used to be a military dictatorship before supposed democracy came back in but it isn't really a democratic country. The President has been there for a very long time. So things are not as outsiders would see.'

When he started to speak in his ordered, concise sentences I knew immediately that he had told this tale before, and had learnt how to shape it. It came as no surprise, near the end of our time together, when he said that telling his story was part of his CBT therapy. As a writer, I know the usefulness of stories when confronting our lives. Stories allow us to structure our experiences into beginning, middle, end, and decide which parts to skim over, which to go into in detail; stories allow us to put forward our own points of view and interpretations; stories, in short, allow us a measure of control over our memories. In lives such as John's, when control is so often in other people's hands, the value of that must be enormous. It must also be difficult to achieve. As we sat together and his tale unfolded, the ordered re-telling began to fracture, gaps appeared, the story doubled back on itself. At various points, John cried. I didn't ask him to fill in gaps or expand on details – the reasons should become clear, if they aren't already.

I am delaying here. I want us to sit with John, the boy who looked at the sky and dreamed of flying through the constellations. But when we met, John did not stop on that any longer than it took to say, 'When I was young, in primary school, my ambition was to become a pilot. So that was my childhood ambition – to be a pilot. But my Dad was involved in politics.' And so we hurtled into the lover's tale.

John's father was not a politician himself, but he financed opposition politicians. This didn't stop John from wanting to join the air force – just as it hadn't stopped his step-brother from joining the army. The route to the skies went through a school that was difficult to get into for anyone who wasn't rich or well connected, but John scored some of the highest marks in the country's national exams and was admitted. The school was close to the army barracks, which meant John went to live with his step-brother, the soldier, who was stationed there.

Soon there was another exam, and John was among those 'selected' at the end of it. Like the others selected with him, he assumed he had scored well – 'We thought, OK, because we're brilliant,' he said, and I briefly glimpsed the confident, bright, would-be pilot – but instead of entering classrooms for the gifted, he and the others were taken to the countryside and made to undergo rituals, such as drinking dogs' blood. They were cadets now, they were told, and each one of them was assigned to an army officer who had them clean their shoes, their houses, and 'do the dirty things that rich people will not do.' They were being taught obedience, and its flip side: fear. At what point, I wonder, did all the brilliant young men who'd been specially selected realise they belonged to the same tribe – the largest tribe of _____, which was not the President's tribe, and from which significant opposition to his rule arose? At what point did they realise they had been selected to spy on, and betray, their own people? 'Gradually we were getting the sense of what was happening,' John told me – gradually, their 'responsibilities' increased from cleaning shoes and accompanying their officers on patrol to befriending people from their own tribe, discovering where their loyalties lay, and reporting them to the authorities if they didn't support the government. Other times, the 'responsibilities' would include planting evidence – 'a pistol, a gun' – in the home of someone they had befriended, just before the police arrived with a warrant to search the house. 'People are picked up and disappeared, they kill them, they do whatever they do to them. I wasn't happy with it. A lot of us weren't happy with it. That wasn't why we were there.'

By now, John's father was dead but his brother had taken up his political activities. It wasn't John but his step-brother, the soldier, who was ordered to bring that brother in for questioning. The step-brother told a friend he wasn't prepared to do it. For this act of familial loyalty he was imprisoned in a room called 'a punishment room'. John, recounting this, gestured around the room we were in, made crowded by a table that could seat at most eight people around it – 'If you divide this room into four, that's the punishment room. You can be in there for weeks.' Within this room, the step-brother fell ill. John was allowed in to see him, and given some medication for him. 'I didn't know it was poison so I gave it to him, and he died.'

★

This is only the beginning.

★

Words like leaves can fall so easily off our tongues, but John had 'nowhere to go', which may be another way of saying 'no way of going.' After he was turned into his brother's killer, he was given several different assignments, moved around from one place to another. Eventually he ended up assigned to one of the sons of the President. He was there when there was a day of celebration in honour of the President. In the evening, after the official celebrations were over, the President's son returned to his house 'to have fun', along with his men, including John.

A woman was brought into a room where the men were gathered. They were ordered to strip her naked. A certain unspeakable indignity was performed. 'It was really, really bad. It was really bad,' John said, his voice very low, and cried for the first time.

The girl was taken away, 'put in a room to die – or whatever happened' and then her brother was brought in. Another unspeakable indignity was performed. 'There was blood everywhere. He was really... emotional.' All this, it later turned out, because the girl hadn't complied with a Presidential demand. So a message had to be sent – to all the girls who might think to refuse such a man, and to all their family members, too.

This was, said John, 'the turning point.' He asked to be re-assigned – if this involved a personal risk he didn't say so; at no point in his story did he pass judgements of praise or criticism on his own actions. He merely recounted events.

He was assigned the job of guarding an elderly couple. He guarded them for 'a very long time,' and as he says, 'the man became like a father to me. He tells me, "you're like a son." He talks to me like a son.' One day when John was with the couple, soldiers came in and shot them dead. 'I thought I'd lost my dad. I was going crazy,' he said, crying again.

The couple had committed no crime. Their son, though, was wanted by the government – John never knew exactly why. The couple were being held to lure the son out of hiding. It didn't work.

And finally – after all the spying, the murder of his brother, the torture of the girl and her brother, the death of his second father – John fled _____, for a life in a country nearby.

★

This is nowhere near the end of the story.

★

Homesickness and hope can be a dangerous combination. John had some kind of life in this other country – he taught at a school to students who taught him English in exchange – but he was lonely, and when there were demonstrations in _____ and the President promised reform, change started to seem

15

possible. John returned to _____, but he kept himself hidden, staying with a friend. On Sundays, though, he went to church. It was here that he met Sarah.

'Met' is the wrong word. They knew each other already. Sarah's father was an important government financier who lived within the protection of the barracks where John had once been posted. John's life was separate from that of Sarah and her family – 'I couldn't talk to them; they were the rich people' – but there was obviously some contact, some connection, because when Sarah saw him she called him by the name he'd had when he was in the barracks. This name was not his traditional name, and it was not the name 'John' which he later took on. It was a name given to him by the army during his initiation, and inscribed on a bangle that he had to wear on his wrist at all times. He was terrified to be recognised, and it couldn't have helped to hear her say that everyone had been looking for him.

He could have run, at this point, though he never said so to me – perhaps it never suggested itself to him as a possibility. Instead, he told her everything. He told her why he had left, and of the loneliness that had brought him home. She was sympathetic. She gave him money. He told her, 'My name is John now.' Every Sunday he would wait for her to come to church. She brought him food and money, and eventually they became, in his words, 'very intimate'.

One day he was standing by the church with two other men when a jeep pulled up, followed by a car. Someone in the car asked, 'Who is John?' He knew, even before this, that something was wrong. Knew it as soon as the car pulled up. Sarah was in the car. She gestured to him to run. But the men caught hold of him and took him back to the barracks. Here he found out that Sarah was pregnant and her father knew.

Her father – the government financier – was angry for reasons beyond the usual reasons that make certain kinds of men angry when they discover their daughters have a life beyond their control. He was a leading member of a tribe that practiced female genital mutilation. But his daughter had not been 'cut', and now he believed her pregnancy would alert people to this fact, and he would be shamed. He wanted the foetus aborted. First though, he came into the cell where John was held, and slapped him. Then he went away but John remained in the cell where he was 'very maltreated.'

While he was being held, Sarah went to a man she knew – a soldier, who was a friend of her father – and told him what was happening. The man said he couldn't stand by while his friend forced an abortion on his daughter, but there was a limit to how much he could – or would – do. He smuggled John out of the barracks in his car, gave him the equivalent of £25, and said, 'Whatever happens to you after is not my problem.' Still, what he did was enough. John met Sarah at a pre-arranged location – a drinking hole – and together they returned to the country to which John had fled.

★

This still isn't near the end of the story.

★

While in exile, John met an American soldier he knew – a logistics expert called Frank who had been assigned to assist the army in _____ when John was serving. He said John should be leading a different life – he suggested emigrating, and offered to help with the costs of getting a visa. Frank's first suggestion was that John go to a particular country in mainland Europe, but John was adamantly opposed to the idea. 'I didn't trust them because I know that whatever happens in _____,

17

they know it; from A to Z they know everything, but they wouldn't stop it. I didn't trust them, I didn't want to go there. I don't want to.' Instead, John went to the British Embassy.

In order to get a visa from the British Embassy, John had to prove he was from the country to which he had fled. The passport that Frank was able to procure for him didn't get past the British visa official who handed him over to the immigration authorities. Once again, he was imprisoned and told he had to stay in a cell while the authorities sorted his case out.

Then, without explanation, he was released. 'Why?' he asked, and they only said, 'You are free to go.'

He walked out of the prison, and a car was waiting for him. He was kidnapped, and driven back to _____.

'That was really horrible. I thought that was it. I really thought that was it. It was difficult for me. They nearly killed me.' At every other point when John cried he carried on speaking through the tears but this time he stopped, apologised, took some time before he was able to continue. It wasn't Sarah's father who had him picked up this time, but someone far worse – the President's son, to whom he had once been assigned. 'He has a house like a stadium, and it has prisons and all the torture things you can think of.' That's all he said the first time, before moving on to the next part of his story. Later, when he had finished his tale, but it was clear there were things still to say, things that he hadn't worked into a narrative over which he had some control, he went back in his mind to that place, to the house like a stadium, with 'all the torture things you can think of' and said some of the things that were done to him. I will not write them here. I'll only say there were many different ways of inflicting pain, and he couldn't have known if it would continue on for weeks or months or years.

After they were done – at what point do torturers decide they are 'done'? – they sent him to an army camp to become a Commando. Perhaps they thought they'd tortured enough fear and obedience into him. The Commandos were men without families, expected to kill or die without a second thought because 'there's no one for you.' He was taken to the Captain of the Commando camp – and the man turned out to be an old friend of his, who had been recruited to the army at the same time as John. John told him he wasn't a man without a family, a man ready to die, but that, instead, he had a wife and a child he needed to get back to. And this friend – 'He just wanted to help me,' John said. 'And so he said, "OK". Well, he put his life at risk for me. He let me go.'

For the third time, John returned to his country of exile.

★

How could this possibly be the end of the story?

★

Because he allowed John to escape, the Captain's hands were placed in wet cement, which was left to dry, and he was dropped into the sea. His dead body washed up on a beach. John received news of this when he was in exile.

★

Frank, the American, must have known that his earlier attempts to get John out of the country had gone disastrously wrong. When John was returned Frank came to him again. This time he had a signed document from a friend who worked in the high court to verify that John had renounced his original nationality and was from his country of exile. With this document, John was able to apply for – and receive – a six month UK visa.

★

This is the beginning of the end of the story, but only the beginning.

★

John's brother – the one who his step-brother was supposed to bring in to the barracks for his role in opposition politics – had long since escaped to mainland Europe and, from there, had come to England. John met up with him, in London, and told him of his intention to apply for asylum. But his brother talked him out of it – he'd applied himself, and been rejected, and was adamant that John couldn't trust the system, never mind how many supporting documents he had. So John moved in with his brother, and didn't seek asylum. His greatest concern was sending money back to Sarah, who by now had had another child. His brother kept saying he would help out, but he didn't, and finally John started to work illegally as a kitchen porter.

One day while he was working, the police arrived and arrested him. 'I told the police officer, what's happening to me? And all the police officers just said to me, "Well, you are one of them." I was put in a car, and they took me to the police station, and I applied for asylum there. By that time, too, I had incontinence through the torture I had back home. They [the men who tortured him] tied my penis and then I had to drink something that makes you want to urinate, but you can't urinate. When that happened I passed out.' John was in prison for six months. From there he was sent to a detention centre and placed on his own in a disabled cell. 'I was on my own,' he said, twice, remembering that time. But he also recalled 'some good people' from his period of detention. In particular, he mentioned a priest who supported him when he thought of killing himself, and who also found people to help him with his incontinence.

His asylum application was rejected. He appealed. An Australian professor, based in America, who had done a lot of work on _____, came to know of his case. This man first spoke to him on the phone and then wrote to the Home Office detailing the situation in _____ and said that if John was sent back there he would be killed. 'He really saved me,' John said. He was granted asylum.

But in all this, John had lost track of Sarah. Their lives in exile had always felt fearful – they moved every month, never let anyone get close enough to ask questions about their lives – and while John was in the UK someone came around to where Sarah was living, asking questions. It was enough to make her flee with her three children – John hadn't known when he left for the UK that Sarah was pregnant again.

In John's tale, there is great brutality but there are also stories of kindness, sometimes from friends and family, sometimes from acquaintances and strangers. A charity in the north of England started to work with Frank who was now back in America, to try and trace Sarah. When they found her where she was exiled she was 'in a hospital, dying.'

Of all the parts in the story that he didn't want to tell this is the one he most completely skimmed over. 'They are here now, they are here,' he said in response to whatever look I gave him when he uttered the word 'dying'. I was left to surmise that someone who is 'dying' in one hospital can turn to 'recovering' in a place with better facilities.

Sarah is well now. She is in England, with John and their three children aged 7, 8 and 11. After all their years of being together, and apart, and together while apart, they married in London. The Church has become their family, and the Bishop who married them is someone they count as a friend. There's even been some kind of rapprochement with Sarah's father. A cousin of Sarah's, who she found via Facebook, was the intermediary in this – when he heard about the wedding he said Sarah should get in touch with her father. She did; she wrote to him about her wedding, and her three children, and he gave her his blessing. They haven't seen each other, but they speak on the phone. And John is a full-time undergraduate maths student in a London university and hopes to be a teacher one day – 'That's all I love doing,' he said. He gestured around the room we were in, which was located on the King's College campus. 'I've applied to a teacher training programme,' he said. 'I'm waiting for the results.'

It isn't easy, though. Torture and imprisonment don't let go of a man that easily – 'I've come a long way,' he said, but the trauma is still there. 'So many things happened to me. I don't like looking at it anymore, I just don't like looking at it anymore.' But the counselling makes him look at it. 'It helps,' he said, 'but it's hard, it's tiring, it's tiring.' Then he started to talk about the torture. Telling me this story brought things up again. But he said again, yes, there are things he has to sort out, but the CBT is helping and he's fortunate in his wife and his family and his church who are supportive of him.

I turned off the recorder, at this point. The story was over, I thought. The life will carry on with its struggles and its hardships, but the worst of it is done, a certain kind of narrative of his experiences has come to an end, and his mind can work towards recovery now. I shook his hand, and thanked him, and then he said – I don't remember how exactly it came up – that earlier in the year he had applied for Indefinite Leave to Remain in the UK, and been denied.

I switched the recorder back on. The whole family applied, he said. His wife and children received Indefinite Leave to Remain but his application was rejected on the grounds he'd been in prison. For working illegally, all those years ago. He would have to wait another 15 years before he could apply again. Surely not another 15 years? He must mean 15 years in total from the time his asylum application was accepted. 'No,' he said, 'it starts this year, so another 15 years.' From his wallet he pulled out the Residence Permits for himself and his children. 'We keep things around,' he said, and I understood he meant that he always had the cards on his person to prove he and his family were legal. The permits for his children all had 'Indefinite Leave to Remain' written on them. Soon they'd be able to apply for citizenship. John's card said 'Refugee Leave to Remain' – he will have to keep re-applying for an extension every 3 years, for the next 15 years. Every re-application bringing with it the threat of a rejection.

'The system is bit...' He doesn't have the words, and neither do I. 'I don't understand it.'

The Abandoned Person's Tale

as told to

Olivia Laing

YOU ARE NOT MUCH more than a boy when it starts. You are a student at a university in the capital city of your country. Let's call that country X. X is a corrupt country, and you are involved in student protests about the elections, which are rigged. A boy running in the streets, a boy high on the notion of freedom. I was also involved in student protests, I remember those feelings.

The student protestors are rounded up, they are arrested, they are taken to the police station. You are very young. The booking policeman is struck by your name, which is the same name as someone powerful in your country. 'Are you related,' he asks. 'Yes,' you say. Leaning close, he tells you what will happen next. He tells you you'll be transferred to a secret prison, an underground prison and if you go there, you will never come out alive. 'He means you are dead,' you tell me.

This man says he will help you. You wait a day in the prison. Unbearable. You wait two days in the prison. Unbearable. That night they come in black jeeps, and load you in. You are alone in your car, you are the only one who is alone. Your jeep swerves away from the convoy, you are taken to a hotel, your relative is there, he takes your photograph. You wait. The next day you are taken to the airport. You are given a new passport.

I am not sending you to France, your relative says. 'I'm going to send you to a country where they have human rights.'

You arrive at Heathrow at 8 in the morning. You don't know what to say, so you put your hand in the air. You don't speak English. The border staff are kind. They give you hot food. They find a translator. Within a week you are living in a flat in London. You are given money by the government. You start a college course. You are the oldest person on the course, it is embarrassing, but you stick with it, you get an A-level, you go on to university, you do a degree. 'This is the 1990s,' you say, 'these things happened.'

The conversation we are having is taking place in London. We have just met, and you are telling me your life story. I hate asking you to tell me this story, because I know you have told it and told it and told it, that you have recited this repertoire of facts, that in some ways you have vanished behind them.

You are wearing a baseball cap. So far, what you are saying is what I expected to hear. I expected you to tell me about a violent, repressive country, about escape. I expected you to tell me about coming to England, my home. I am pleased about the hot meal, the flat, the education. 'Yes,' I think, 'you did well to come here, to a country with human rights.'

And then your story changes direction. It starts with a mistake, a stupid error of judgement. You buy a plasma television from an acquaintance. It is very cheap, but you don't think too much about that. The next thing you know, the police are at your door. You are arrested, you are sentenced for receiving stolen goods. You go to prison, far away, in a part of the country you don't know. Well then. Head down, you serve your time. You are released. 'Oh my dear,' you say to me sadly, 'that's the beginning of disaster now.'

Outside the prison, the border guards are waiting for you. They are holding a big photograph of you, you can't escape it. While you were inside, the law changed. If you are sentenced for more than a year, you are automatically a subject for deportation. You served nine months, but your sentence was for 18. You are a subject for deportation.

Now the nightmare starts. Every month a report is written. It says bad things about you. What, I ask and you say you will be considered 'more than the devil, the devil even is good.'

Then the detention centre is burned down. They have to put you somewhere, so they put you back in prison. 'I am not a prisoner, I'm only a detainee,' you tell them, but it takes four months before they release you. The first condition of your liberty is that you must be tagged. The second condition is that you have a curfew. The third condition is that you must report to the border authority three times a week. The fourth condition is that you cannot work. A return ticket to the place where you have to report is £24. You have to report three times a week. You cannot work. 'Miss, life is hard,' you tell me. 'Life is hard.'

'They want to force you to go back?' I ask. 'To frustrate you,' you say. 'To damage you. To finish your life.'

After a year of this, you ask if you can sign at your local police station. 'No,' you are told. 'That is absolutely not possible.'

'Okay, if this is the case, I will stop signing because I can't, I can't,' you tell them. 'The day you arrest me is up to you guys.'

A year goes by. Then one day you are on a bus. You are reading the *Metro*. Three boys get on the bus and they steal your phone. You ask the driver to stop the bus. 'Driver, please, it's my only contact,' you say. The police come. They get your phone back, but then, *bango*, they realise you are wanted by immigration, that you have absconded. The superintendent himself comes out to tell you that the Home Office will pick you up in the morning.

You go back to a detention centre. This time, you are made an orderly. You are paid £25 a week to look after the new detainees. You are allowed to work in here, an irony that doesn't escape you.

Three years go by. Here is what you say about those years. You are crying now.

'I see people, nine month, they are trying to hang themself, nine month, but me three years [pause] It was not easy. It was not easy, miss. [pause] I try my best to be a man [pause] the suffering that I endure psychologically, miss, if I give it to you, you commit suicide – you cannot take it. No human people can take it. Even your dog cannot take it. But I took it. Do you know how many people they wanted to commit suicide in this detention centre? Detention is not good. Detention give birth to [pause] hatred.'

Your case goes to trial seventeen times. On the eighteenth time, the judge is kind. He tells you to pack your bag. He tells you that you are being released.

You are released, but you still aren't at liberty. You cannot sleep. You do not like to be around people, you feel afraid of them. Sometimes you hear voices that tell you to kill yourself. Sometimes you talk out loud. You are depressed. You think maybe you are dreaming, that nothing is very real. You still can't work, you still have to sign every week, you still don't have indefinite leave to remain.

Soon, in a few days, that might change. 'Almost there,' I say, and you say bitterly, 'it's not about almost there, it's half of my age. Two decades and a half.'

I don't know when I have ever felt so ashamed. I think of you as a boy, running in the street, high on the notion that you can change your country, can make it better. You have not had a life. Your life has been wasted, thrown away.

What has happened to you has happened here, on British soil. 'I'm sorry,' I say, but no words can help. What I would like to give you is time: 1303 weeks, 9125 days, 219,000 hours, a quarter century stolen from you.

That is what detention is: a thief of talent, of energy, of time. For weeks I think of your uncle, standing at the airport, saying, 'I am sending you to a country with human rights.'

What has been done to you cannot be undone, what has been taken from you cannot be returned. All the same, we could become that country. We could as a nation stop being so lethally afraid of strangers, so dangerous in our self-protection.

You are a Christian and I am not, but we both agree on this: kindness is what counts. So imagine a country founded on kindness, a country that treats desperate strangers with respect. And now we come to the question that haunts me. What could you have become in that good, imagined place? What would you have done with your beautiful life?

The Walker's Tale

as told to

Ian Duhig

'ONLY THOSE WHO ARE lost in error follow the poets' goes my
   Abdel Haleem
version of the untranslatable Qur'an; 'See how they rove
   aimlessly…
how they say what they do not do.' I'm about to prove God's
   point. Again.

In another kind of show, this would be the prologue or an
   antimasque,
a suggestion of what this tale means but that retreats from me
   endlessly,
a mirage, even its sentences indefinite, suspended or deferred.

For reasons, the Walker wears a mask here so I must mind my
   words
as he once minded his animals in an African village I won't
   name either.
'Mask' comes from '*maskhara*', Arabic, which the Walker speaks,

a Latin to his world like French once or English now, invader
   languages.
Roads are tongues, but this is no easy Chaucerian ride or stroll:
   its feet aren't
poetic: they blister, trip over the wrong end of the stick, get lost

mapping roots of words as if escape routes, so for this moving tale,
we track 'metaphor' from 'a carrying over' onto Greek pantechnicons now,
then to wondering if it's used in translating 'Immigration Removal Centre'.

'Translate' was 'carry across', like a tune between lines, 'Lili Marlene',
or the Syrian exile Adonis' poem 'Music', borne into the English language
by Mattawa: 'In this house an immigrant lives and his name is meaning.'

I wondered if Adonis punned there on *beit* as both 'house' and verse unit: poets
homeless between writing poems in Celan's conception, as it were,
but even I had tact enough not to ask the Walker his views about that.

His own name derives from 'Rightly-guided' in one of his many languages,
but our paths crossed not on pilgrimage to Mecca, Rome, Jerusalem
or Canterbury, but while visiting The Theatre of Dreams at Old Trafford.

Under the big poster of its legends there, he talked about ginger Scholes
and ginger coffee made at home so strong that if you drink it once,
you'll crave it at that same time every day forever. Guests loved it.

They loved guests at home, a chance to show they rose above animals, that they
weren't barbarians. We talked about this, then about other things.

On my train home I made notes as full of his silences as his
    words,

their white songlines as beyond me to conduct as flocks he
    guided
through a landscape war changed constantly, where one day's
    fields
were battlefields the next under the flies' black flags and
    lamentations.

He sighed, 'My story is too long.' So he cut to the chase, his own
by Janjaweed, a militia whose name means mounted jinn,
    demon cavalry charged
with rooting out traitors, or who they say are traitors. One day,

cars scream up and men spill out bristling with guns and
    questions: Where does
he think he is going? Who does he think he is?
Why does he support the enemy? Why is he a traitor? Why does
    he lie?

The Walker answered, I support only my family and Manchester
    United.
They drove him off anyway and tortured him for weeks, maybe
    months,
the first time he learns that water can be his enemy, can be a
    weapon.

Eventually, his torturers get bored, his abuse too routine to
    interest them,
the Walker's family too poor for any chance of a decent ransom.
Security slackened. Describing his escape over their compound
    wall,

the Walker said he was lucky. He said this many times when we
    spoke,

meaning lucky he's not currently being tortured, burned,
    drowned or shot,
lucky he's only waiting for something terrible to happen now, all
    the time.

He was free then and there, but home meant Janjaweed
    vengeance.
He needed to get money to his family now and that meant a
    city.
He didn't know which way to turn, like an animal cut from the
    herd.

A bookherd, I'd turn to Sterne's gift of his many-handled
    walking stick, boxing
the compass while standing still, all the world's roads unrolling
from its pointless point like Rome or ink. I pen my stock, but
    my mind

wanders, grazing on the '*Kitab al-'Asa*', Usamah's walking stick
    anthology, Solnit
on that African tribe's Hajj deferring arrival at Mecca
    indefinitely, Schopenhauer
on our every step a fall deferred like Galeano's Utopia:

'I go two steps, she moves two steps away... I'll never reach her.
What good is utopia? That's what it's good for, walking.' Utopia
    means no-place,
although the Walker didn't need me to translate that for him.

Because he can mind animals, he gets a lift moving herds to
    Libya,
'A migrant slave market on the world's most dangerous refugee
    route'
in the words of the TV journalist who followed in the Walker's
    footsteps.

Here the Walker is penned up indefinitely in no country for old
  men,
women, the young, the unarmed, those who can be sold in part
  or whole.
Here, you need to carry a big stick or loaded gun, since our side
  won.

The Walker fled one militia in the Janjaweed, but Libya has
  hundreds
permanently prowling the streets in pick-up trucks with anti-
  aircraft guns,
no other ways of making money in peace and families of their
  own to feed.

Step outside your detention centre, get kidnapped; stay in, get
  beaten,
abused, starved. Because he can mind animals, he's taken to a farm,
a blank on his driver's map, a no-place where time soon lost
  itself.

After forever, he asks for money pay to send home, earning only
  blows
and threats from the farm owner. So the Walker began to walk
  again, heading for
where he heard real jobs waited, under the Northern Star.

Now he draws a blank by design for the next level of his turning
  hell:
the Sahara, the page that eats all tales, the winds that drown all
  song.
Walking through this hourglass means death, but work lies on
  routes

worn by eight centuries of caravans of black slaves and
  concubines before the
Walker and his new fellow travellers, from Sudan, meaning

'Land of Blacks', and young Nigerian girls making their own
    false friends.

I've seen the journalist's footage of smugglers' convoys on this
    route:
it's 'Mad Max' in cattle trucks battering along flat out for fear of
    the tribes,
old, young, men and women hanging off their ropes like ragged
    flags.

As lucky, the Walker swung from a wing mirror for days
    knowing if he fell,
only death would kindly stop for him. Sweat oils fingers.
    Muscles burn.
Winds whistle and cut like swords. You only need one more
    distraction:

a sudden bump, a cry; a spray of white sand then distance and
    mirages swallow
people whose names the Walker still remembers, his silences
still their elegies here, their shrouds surrounding every letter on
    this page.

Arabic has forty words for sand, sixty for sword, seventy for water
but none for what the Walker wanted to tell. What was his boat
    like?
He shrugged, gesturing at the rickety bookcase bodged up from
    a kit.

Who'd go to sea in such? People who know the risks they are
    taking,
who know they'll have only enough fuel to reach international
    waters,
who write phone numbers on their clothes so their bodies
    might be known.

On the beach, the Walker saw patched thirty-foot rubber
 dinghies,
heard them still hissing like promises after their pumps were
 uncoupled
and thought, at least wood floats. Five hundred crammed into his
 boat.

Its builder looked on and shook his head till pistol-whipped. On
 this coast,
fishermen haul up with their catches skulls like white glass net
 floats.
This boat's ribs creaked. It wasn't caulked. Taking to sea, it took
 on water.

The Walker bailed with a sieve of his clothes, seeing reflections
 of those lost in
the Sahara clinging on here but to gunwale-ropes not truck
 straps.
They fall away always, forever out of reach, mirages made of real
 water.

He found himself treading water instead of sand, his hourglass
 time dissolving
again till he heard a sound at first frightening, like feasting flies,
but slowly rising to a warm growl. A searchlight stopped on
 their wreck.

Through shuddering down-draughts, a steel angel dropped
 lifejackets.
Coastguard hauled survivors aboard, wrapped them in foil
 blankets
although the Walker still shivered as he told me again how he
 was lucky.

Landed on the boot of Italy, his ground would never feel solid
 again.

Welcomes melted as fast as prospects of work. Like the
    Janjaweed,
Frontex acted as if he was their enemy. Paradise found is paradise
    lost.

The whorls and eddies of the Walker's fingerprint are now his
    signature
to European power, his spoken tale attended to only for
    inconsistencies, his
identity doubted or denied. They gave the barefoot Walker flip-
    flops

and handbooks, so he read with his feet like Ovid in the
    Sulmonese legend
or Dante finding paradise along the lines of Arab poets' night
    journeys,
Ibn Shuhay, Ibn al-'Arabi and Al-Ma'arri whose faith he
    consigned to Hell.

'*Traduttore, traditore*', the translator is a traitor, they say in that
    country,
if not just about translators now. The Walker didn't need a Bible
    to translate
the writings on the wall outside his hostel and set off for work
    again.

He'd walk all night, reeling between the film-strips of railway
    lines.
In his dream, he headed north but his feet turned towards home,
    south. Now the Walker
began to lose trust even in his own walking and the stars.

The Walker learned to ride any vehicle, any way, even upside-
    down
through Italy then into France. In Calais, he saw a Sudanese
    refugee

try to ride an articulated lorry upside-down and die. He hadn't
   asked how.

The Walker hung on to reach England but, his dream realised at
   last,
he just passed out on the oasis of the motorway central
   reservation,
sleeping till arrested, printed, processed and again detained
   indefinitely.

Home Office staff brooded over his fingerprints as if contour
   maps unspooling
from Italy, so they sent him back there, without notice,
tied up like a corpse: feet foremost, carried over, carried across
   only

to be driven north again by his hunger for work, money for his
   family.
Here, the Walker will live in more English cities than I have all
   my life,
including my home now, Leeds, known as the Jerusalem of the
   North,

in antisemitic abuse because of all the Jews who fled here once,
many from Cossack Janjaweed. Their grateful children raised in
   thanks
the plaque on Oakwood Clock where the Walker could catch a
   bus to see

the memorial arch raised by grateful children of Huguenot
   réfugiés
whose first gift to us was the word 'refugee'. Their arch's
   keystone reads:
'*Aimez votre prochain comme vous-même.*' The past is a foreign
   country

without border controls. Strangely, the Walker has become a
    guide here, as Leo Africanus
for Jonson's masque or Yeats' poetry. A traitor to some, Leo was
Berber, people named from the same abuse in Arabic as Greek

'Barbarian': *bar bar bar*, foreigners babbling like frightened
    flocks
the Walker might calm if allowed but that's neither here nor
    there, like he is,
officially, living between the lines on our traffic island, barred
    from work,

unheard at his own hearings, their indefinite sentences
    unservable, endless
mirages of legal Latin babble. I babble here, trying to conjure
    up
for you how it can be that one day out walking, the world just
    turns

against you, first in your own country and then everywhere you
    go,
how rising cries of bar, bar, bar drowned all the Walker's
    languages,
whose own real name could hurt him if I were to speak it here,

how stones were given him instead of bread, sticks broke his
    bones
which might have shown him the way, helped him walk or
    traced in sand
its forty Arabic names, the ninety-nine of God, the Walker's
    millions.

He walks on, every day a step, a fall deferred in a deferred life.
    I've heard some
people say the Walker's kind are here because we were there:

'The man in boots walks where he likes' as the Irish proverb
    explains.

'I have fled through land and sea, blank land and sea, / Because
    my house is
besieged by murderers...' Kafka's first translator voices refugees:
    'Here without
blame, yet with blame, / Dark blame of other.' Blame

my version of the Walker's untranslatable tale on many counts:
lack of direction, poetry, closure or definition, in the last as bad
    as UK law for leaving
you in the dark, which I do again now my curtain falls here,

reminding me of Szymborska's 'Utopia': 'Island where all
    becomes clear
Solid ground beneath your feet. The only roads those that offer
    access... On the right
a cave where Meaning lies.' Utopia. No place. Home.

The Witness' Tale

as told to
Alex Preston

Home

YOU REMEMBER LITTLE OF the time before you came to your country's capital city. You were born in the east, where a decades-long war still simmered. All you could recall of that place was sunlight, warmth, cooking smells on heavy evening air. You were five when your father moved your family to the city. In the capital, you lived by the sea in a row of ancient, colonial houses that once were white but had now taken on the colour of the sand. You spent all the time you weren't at school in the dusty streets between the rows of houses, playing the local sport, a complicated game with paddles and a ball and much shouting. You grew as a tree might grow, in sudden, surprising bursts followed by years in which you hardly seemed to change at all. Let's call you V.

This was the start of things, V. You were sitting at home aged sixteen, studying, or attempting to study. Your father was at his barber shop in the city centre, a city that was twitchy, on edge after a series of bomb blasts. At four-thirty, your father came home unexpectedly with news that your cousin, R, who worked as your father's assistant, had been arrested. He was a suspect, your father said, in one of the bomb blasts. They believed that your cousin was a member of the insurgency. You knew that he was innocent, a more innocent, studious boy could not be imagined.

After a few days your father finally managed to get your cousin's case brought before a magistrate. The magistrate said that, since there wasn't any evidence against him, the police could only hold him for fourteen days. During those days, R was tortured by the police. This was very common where you come from. Then your mother gave her jewels to the police officer in charge of the station where he was being held and your cousin was released. This, too, was common.

You should say here that your father's older brother was once a member of the insurgency. This was long ago, and the war was another war, nobler and less complex than the war now. The uncle had fled abroad, and R was not his son, but rather the son of your father's sister. Still, a few days later, the police arrived at your house again, although this time with them were four army officers. They asked very politely where your father was. He's upstairs, you said, but your father had heard the cars outside and was descending the staircase already.

They took you away, you and your father and your poor, broken cousin, all with your hands bound and black hoods over your heads. You weren't especially worried, even then. Everything had the tentative air of a dream, and anyway, you were in the capital city. People disappeared in the east, where you were born, but not here, not in the shadow of the newly-built World Financial Centre, under the benevolent gaze of UN inspectors.

You were taken to a police station and placed in three separate rooms. They were surprised at how well you spoke their language, for although you used the language of the east with your family, you had learnt the tongue of the capital city and spoke it with the conviction of a native of that place. They told you that your father had confessed, that he'd confessed to them he was a long-time member of the insurgency. Your cousin, too, they said, was a leader of the terrorists' youth wing. You laughed. 'I know nothing of this,' you said. Then they began to beat you. 'I don't know anything,' you said, as they went in first with their fists, then with a black rod which they used upon your ribs, your shins, your ankles, employing more and more force until things started to break and burst. 'I don't know anything,' you insisted. You still have hard places that should be soft because of those beatings.

Much later, a police officer came in, this one kinder, gentler than the others. 'I want my mother,' you said. He allowed you to telephone her, told you which station you were being held in so you could say it down the line to your mother. She went to your local MP, a good man. The MP sent his private secretary to the jail. She couldn't get your father and brother out, but you were released because you were a schoolboy. Then the MP told your mother the name of a certain person, the friend of a judge, to whom money could be brought, who would pass on supplications. Your mother sold the last of her jewellery and the next day your father and cousin were home.

Everything had changed, though. It was a close community you lived in and news travelled fast up and down those dust-blown streets. After your arrest, your neighbours looked at you as if you were terrorists. More often, they did not look at you at all. You sat at home and listened to the shouts of the boys playing the local sport, the way their voices would rise in vexation or joy, and you wished that you could be out there with them, running, running, through the dust and sea-tang air.

Three days later and the final blow fell. M, your brother, was twelve. He was a tubby, bespectacled kid, always hanging round your mother, always with his finger in something in the kitchen. He was smart, too, as near the top of his class as you were near the bottom of yours. The army had heard that you'd been released and came to your school looking for you. You were off that day, sick. The principal of the school tried to put up a fight. He told the army officers that they weren't allowed to come into the school. They just laughed at him. They said that he was hiding insurgents. The principal called you over the school's intercom. When you didn't come he told them that you had a younger brother, and he called M.

The army officers left no word about where they had taken M. The principal called your father and you went down to the school with him. You and your father visited all of the police stations of the capital city, but none of them was holding him. They told you that the army had taken him, not the police; you needed to apply to go to army headquarters. You and your father tried to get written permission, but were repeatedly refused. M was never seen again, not by you, or your father, or by your mother, who loved him so very much.

Departure

Your father sent you to live with an aunt, up in the mountains where the air was fresh and green, flowers twining around the buildings and terraces stepping down the hillsides. You stayed there for three months and then your father sent for you. Life once again took on a dream-like aspect, a feeling of inevitability. Your father explained very little, but the day after your return to the city, he took you to sit your English Language exams. You could hardly speak a word – it was your least favourite subject at school – but you sat down, filled in the question sheet willy-nilly and handed it in.

Later, your father would tell you that he had a customer in the barber shop, a white man. He'd explained everything to this man, about the police and the army, about the beatings, about M. The man and his wife would help to get you out of the country, to find you asylum in the UK. The man's wife met with you after the exam. She was very kind, very softly spoken. She told you that you would receive a high grade in your exam, that she'd transfer money to your father's bank account, that you would leave to start a new life in England.

The airport, the plane, your father hurrying you along, disguising emotion with bustle. You'd said goodnight to your mother the night before. And then, before you knew it, you were rising, turning, a long bank which afforded you a last look at the sunset city below, a futile attempt to pick out your house, somewhere along the dimly glowing shore-line. Then you were gone, up and up through clouds and into the vastness of the air.

Abroad

You are met by a friend of your father's at Heathrow. They haven't seen each other in a decade or more, but the man is kindly and cheerful, takes your bag and laughs when you marvel at his Sat Nav. He drives you to Leicester. The roads are wide and endless and grey. You meet his wife, you settle in to life there. Once a week, you take the National Express coach to London. The £300 your father gave you spends itself with terrifying speed. In London you go to a college in Lewisham that claims to offer classes in English and business studies, computer technology and marketing. It's entirely chaotic – you see that immediately. The staff lounge outside smoking, or loll about with their feet on their desks. If you pay your fees, you get a certificate. It's a con and you want no part of it.

Here begins a part of your story where you seem to lose all agency, V. Others use you and you appear easily used. Your father's friend seems suddenly exasperated by your presence. He drives you to a large house in Harlesden where there is a woman from your country who offers you a bed. It's a small and sad little room, the smell of dampness, stains on the walls. Your father's friend says he's going to buy you a new mattress and duvet. He never comes back. You go to a payphone and call his mobile again and again, you leave messages until your coins run out. The lady from your country says you can stay for a week, two at the most. Soon, it is your eighteenth birthday, and you spend it in the sad little room on your own. You have almost none of your father's money left.

You find a job at Sand Valley Restaurant, a place run by people from your own country. They say they can't employ you legally, but you can work as an illegal. They'll pay you £1.50 an hour. Your job is cleaning, 6pm-6am. You do two weeks, non-stop, twelve hours each night, sleeping during the day. When you ask for your wages, the manager says that the first week was your training period – unpaid. So for two weeks' work you are given just over £100. You're furious, you say to yourself that you must find another job, but everywhere you go on your long hopeless daytime wanderings the people say they can't employ illegals.

Then, one evening, the manager of Sand Valley, where you're still, grudgingly, working, tells you that there are four men from the east of your country there. You go and sit with them, and it is such a pleasure to pour out your story, to chew over those words that are like memories in your mouth. You tell them everything, and the three men nod and hum and shake their heads, and tell you that your story is sad and familiar. You should be in France, they say, where asylum seekers are looked after so well. Or Germany, where you would be given money by the State, your own apartment, training for a job. One of the men, short, with a scraggy moustache, says that he runs an agency that helps people escape the UK, which is a cruel, cold and unwelcoming place, to find shelter on the Continent. Here you risk deportation, the Agent claims, flights are leaving Heathrow every day taking people back to our country. One-way ticket.

You go home, collect your belongings, say goodbye to the woman, who is surprisingly sad that you are leaving, and clutches your hands as you go. You stay with the Agent, who lives in a large house in Cricklewood, all plasma televisions and glass coffee tables and beds with thick duvets. His wife is pregnant and cooks you dinner, a traditional dish of the east. You sleep better that night than you have since coming to England, knowing that you will soon be in safer, more welcoming hands.

The next night, the other men from the restaurant come to dinner. They ask to see your passport, try to persuade you to change it for a false one. You refuse. Later, the Agent asks you to let him have your passport so that he can obtain the visa required to enter France. This time you let him take the passport. Early one morning, you and the Agent set off in his car. It is dark and the dashboard glows blue and red. He takes you to a McDonald's and buys you whatever you want. Finally you arrive at Folkestone, ready to board the Chunnel. The English customs officials wave you through, then you come to French passport control. The Agent holds up his passport and yours, smiles thinly. The French officer looks at them, looks again. He asks the Agent to pull the car into a parking bay.

They take you into separate rooms. It's only later that you learn that the Agent has shown them a false passport. 'Was that your passport he showed us,' the official asks, his accent difficult for you to understand. 'Yes,' you say, 'yes it was,' because you don't know. And it seems hard to believe, but this is one of the defining moments of your life, a mistake that will haunt the days, months and years to come.

They arrest you both, put you in a room together. 'Listen,' the Agent says to you, 'I did something bad. I swapped the passports. I'm sorry. I need yours, for someone else, someone in a desperate situation. Please don't tell the police. I have a baby coming and they'll lock me away. If you say it was your passport, and that you're only eighteen, they'll put you in jail for a week, ten days maximum. Please, V, haven't I been kind to you? Please do this for me. I know so many police officers. I'll pay them to release you.'

And V, you do it, because you're good and you're innocent. The customs officers and policemen who interview you seem at first bemused, then angry with you. Finally one, an older man, comes in, and says, 'Did you try to come into France under false documentation?' And you say 'Yes, yes I did.' You go before a judge in Brighton, who gives you a sentence of one year with automatic deportation. You're sent to Elmley Prison, out on the marshes, where you feel life falling away from you, everything sinking into the cold wet earth. Then you meet an interpreter, E, who is kind to you. You tell her the truth about the Agent and the passports and the terrible mistake, and she shakes her head sadly and tells you that, since you've admitted your guilt, there's nothing you can do.

After two weeks at Elmley, they transfer you to Rochester Young Offenders' Institute. You've been scared, have heard dark stories of racism and bullying, but it is a fine place. You make friends with the other boys, who are kind to you, fascinated by your history, your tales of your country, don't seem to notice that you are the only one amongst them with dark skin. You garden, you study, you read books about Lenin and Gandhi, books that were banned in your country lest they foment the spirit of revolution amongst the people.

The police officers come to see you again. They tell you that the Agent is actually a people smuggler. That he has been raping women, trafficking them for sex, that he runs people from England to France, then picks up people in France whom he smuggles to England. They say that if you help them it will be good for your appeal. 'Will you be a witness?' You say, of course, of course you will.

Now a string of appeals, nine detention centres in two years, each as faceless and labyrinthine as the last. Colnbrook is, perhaps, the worst. If you take a shower, your room floods. You complain about it and they tell you to put up with it, or you'll get a red mark on your file. Prison was better than this. You listen to all of the stories of the people there, because you've stopped telling your own story so freely. There are detainees from Sudan, from Congo, from Nigeria. People who had lost their children and were half-mad with grief, young people who'd seen their parents die before them. You lie in bed at night and you hear sighs and muffled sobs, you imagine their stories roaming the corridors of that place. You've never been anywhere so sad.

More setbacks, more trouble. You've a cast-iron asylum case, you're told, but you're a criminal, and criminals are a harm to the public. You'll be deported, there's no question. Then you receive a letter from Legal Aid, saying that they cannot continue to support your case. Again, you feel life slipping away from you. You try to imagine yourself back in your homeland and you find that your appetite, your energy, your ability to get to sleep at night, all these have deserted you.

E, the interpreter, hears that you've lost Legal Aid. She comes to see you. 'I've just qualified as a lawyer,' she says. 'You can be my first case.' She's been speaking about you to her husband, a police officer. Her husband believes your story. 'He's a fool, is V,' he says, 'but he's innocent.' You are granted bail, although you must keep to a curfew, must wear an electronic tag around your leg. You move through a series of lonely government accommodation centres, then E finds you a place down south, near Portsmouth.

The police come to you again. The people-smuggling gang will be tried at Maidstone Crown Court. You'll have to give evidence, they tell you, you can do it by video link, your face hidden, the traffickers won't see your face. But, due to some clerical or administrative error, you aren't hidden away but must speak in front of the gang. The Agent is right there, sitting forward and looking straight at you with murderous eyes. You speak to a girl just before you go in to the courtroom. She'd been raped by the Agent, and she thanks you for speaking out. Her words give you bravery and so you tell the truth about the passport, about your time with the Agent. They get seven or eight years each. As they walk out, they shout in the language of your home that they will find you and kill you. That wherever you go in the world, they will hunt you down and kill you like a dog.

Now, you live in limbo, negotiating the warrens and blind alleys of bureaucracy. You are twenty-three, twenty-five, twenty-seven. Appeals and counter-appeals have been heard and rejected. Appeals to the Home Office, to the Criminal Cases Review Commission. You are passed from one court to the next, you are offered hope and then this hope is snatched away. Years have passed and soon the smugglers will be free. The police thank you, and even the Home Office write you a letter of gratitude, apparently unaware that they are seeking to deport you. They tell you they will protect you, but you know that the smugglers have links in your home country. They will either get you here or there, you think. You wake scared in the mornings. You speak only to a handful of friends. You try not to speak too much. You have started to look behind you when you're out walking. Your life is passing, V, you realise this, and eventually one appeal will be the final appeal, and a decision will be made, and at least that will be some kind of ending.

The Barrister's Tale

as told to

Rachel Holmes

'WHY IS THE BEAVER making laces? Mum, don't fall asleep. Finish the story.'

'She's tired love; we'll let her be.'

Face down on the couch, beside a half-empty bottle of red wine. Always red wine with me. Whisky gives me the glums. And, worse, makes me feel like a cliché. But today was a good day. They happen. Sometimes.

> 'I'll read to you Sprout. Pass the book.'
> They sought it with thimbles, they sought it with care;
> They pursued it with forks and hope;
> They threatened its life with a railway-share;
> They charmed it with smiles and soap.
>
> But the Barrister, weary of proving in vain
> That the Beaver's lace-making was wrong,
> Fell asleep, and in dreams saw the creature quite plain
> That his fancy had dwelt on so long.

'What's wrong with the Beaver's shoelaces?'

'Nothing. He doesn't wear shoes. He's making lace - like um... fancywork for clothes or tablecloths or webs or nets.'

'Fancy Work? Like Mum being a Barista?'

Her favourite joke. Every day.

'Explain about the wrong lace that's not for shoes.'

Oh I'm so glad you have to try and unpick that and not me. Tonight I'm just a knackered happy instrument of truth, an advocate of social justice, the epitome of reason. My own little Atticus Finch. Replaying the jubilant relief in his voice in my silent disco.

'The Beaver is making a sort of fabric called lace, formed by weaving thread in patterns. It's delicate material, open, made of lots of pretty gaps and holes.'

Not bad. Though you've told her what not why. I'm looking forward to you explaining to her where the Snark lives. She asked me three times last night. I said wait and see. Today was a videolink Tribunal, relayed from Brook House detention centre. I couldn't even give Omar a smile when the judge said she'd decided to grant bail. But he shouted his thanks as he was being brought out; and I could hear the smile and light in his voice. Relief. Actual joy. They took him out fast so the next one could come in. They're very efficient with time in videolink cases. Shows they can be when they want to. The next one was up immediately. Today was our day though. One we won.

It's been much better with Faiz since I stopped bringing it home so much. He's picking up the slack for me. Quite the house husband. Talking with that writer who interviewed me over lunch in Coopers for the Refugee Tales project the other day, I suddenly realised how hard I try not to think about it except when I'm doing it. Or speak about it, except with colleagues.

I'm not the story.

I said in my email that we could go to one of the Inns for lunch if she liked – sometimes people want to get a feel of the pomp of barrister's places – but it's not really where refugee lawyers generally eat. Coopers is very handy for my chambers. I'd rather have my comfort food served with geniality than pretention. That sounds pretentious. I ordered fish pie and we got through the introductions. I was raised in Ireland during the troubles; she grew up in apartheid South Africa. So we understood each other well enough, that saved time. No need to explain why I became what other people call a human rights lawyer and what I think of as the only kind of lawyer I could ever become.

She'd visited an immigration detention centre, derided the prohibition on taking in pen and notebook. I grimaced. 'Well,' she said, tapping her head with her breadknife, 'G4S haven't got hold of the switch for turning off the recording device in my brain — yet.' We talked about my training and I told her I did some English literature with my law and we discovered we're both Ray Bradbury fans.

I was hungry, looking forward to the pie. Faiz had started his course that morning; I did Sprout's breakfast and the school run and grabbed a coffee on the way to Lincoln's Inn. Before the food arrived we started talking about the hostile language of immigration law. Temporary indefinite detention. How do you measure time that's both temporary and indefinite? That's a question for Stephen Hawking, not an answer to the rules of human law supposed to protect and help people who need refuge, care and hope.

Indefinitely temporary: temporarily indefinite. Holding people prisoners of language. Prisoners have proper sentences, that can be counted down, marking the days off on a five bar gate that opens when the time is done. But our detainees face unlimited days that can only be counted upwards without the end in sight. You're trying to count the trees in a dark wood but find you're in a tangled forest of a thousand demons unable to get out, and either no one can hear you calling for help or they're ignoring you.

Waiting indefinitely to be removed imminently. It's like Beckett and Orwell met for a bender on Bloomsday in The Kafka's Head.

She asked about the process. How we prepare the cases. The circs under which we interview people. What do I do? 'Tell me,' she said, 'the sort of questions you would ask in an interview with a client to prepare an asylum application. Let's say, for example, your case is a student from Daraa, active in the Syrian protest movement. What makes a fear of persecution well founded?'

I had quite a lot of those outside court, particularly in 2011 and 2012. My conferences with clients would generally be before the hearing of an asylum appeal – sometimes just before. All of the meaty questions would have been asked by the solicitors when taking the witness statements and preparing clients for interviews. The questions I ask are based on whatever is in the refusal letter that hasn't been ironed out sufficiently in the statement for the hearing. Typically I ask questions I intend to ask at the appeal to find out what the answer is first – so I don't ask a question that I don't already know the answer to. Although I have occasionally had a client make up an entirely new claim on the spot so completely that I can't help but join them on the voyage of creative discovery. She laughed and said, 'I'm definitely using that.'

A first-time asylum seeker would not usually be detained for long. They would pretty much always have been released by the time of an asylum appeal.

If we were having a conference in advance in chambers, which aren't terribly common but do happen in complex cases or with vulnerable clients, I would have been asking a lot of the questions.

We ate in silence whilst she read my sample document. A life in a list.

'The Home Office says that you would be safe in another part of Syria – is there anywhere else you could go to? If not why not?'

'The Home Office says that it is not credible that you would have decided to oppose the government given your family's background - why do you say it is?'

'The Home Office says that you would be safe if you stopped your activities against the government – why don't you do that?'

'The Home Office says you should have reported your harassment to the authorities – how do you respond?'

'The Home Office says it's not credible that you could have travelled safely from Daraa to the UK if you were wanted – what do you say to that?'

'The Home Office says that if you were really at risk you would not have been able to hide for 3 months in your uncle's basement - what do you say to that?'

'The Home Office says that you are speculating that your friend gave your name under torture – why do you believe this?'

'The Home Office says that you could have received your injuries as a result of something other than torture – how do you respond to that?'

She circled all the interrogatives with her pencil as she read.

> *If not why not?*
> *Why do you say it is?*
> *Why don't you do that?*
> *How do you respond?*
> *What do you say to that?*
> *Why do you believe this?*
> *How do you respond to that?*

I forged on, and told her that, in fact, I generally spend a lot of those meetings just being nice to clients to try and make them at ease with the process, and only asking a few questions not dealt with by solicitors. The solicitors who are committed and diligent enough to ask for a conference with me are often the ones who have already prepared the case so well my counsel is virtually superfluous. 'Do you think the way you talk?' she interrupted, but I was still answering the last question.

I most often meet clients for the first time outside Tribunal, possibly in a conference room if we can find one, or sitting on a couple of chairs, or just standing in a corner away from others. Solicitors frequently do the job of going to the detention centres. I've had a number of clients I've represented for years, gotten out of detention on contested applications after an all-day row in the High Court, but who I never actually met because for High Court cases clients aren't usually produced. 'So,' she said, 'I've spent more time with you over this lunch than you do with many of the individuals who you're under all this daily pressure to represent. You have to read the brief and prepare the argument and go in to try and make an intervention in the life of someone wholly depersonalised by a system that treats them like suspicious and unwanted and threatening strangers. Our welcome to Britain. You have to embody their human appeal. You know their stories. You're the voice.'

Faiz says that human rights lawyers have the hardest, most complex stories to tell and that he thinks what I do is heroic and admirable. I love him for being a dedicated romantic. He believes human rights are about Shelley and retaining idealism and not just what we have to do to negotiate a baseline of shared decency and solidarity when all the idealism's unravelled. My college friends who chose financial law like to call themselves sceptics and lord it over me at reunions with their worldly cynicism. Yet they go to work in the City every morning in a system they know is designed to work for them. Refugee lawyers graft in a system redesigned to work against us in a legal environment becoming more hostile by the day. There've been eight immigration bills in the last eight years and over 45,000 changes to the immigration rules since 2010. There's a new challenge at every turn. And even where it isn't entirely against us, we're required to dance harder and faster.

When we went through that really bumpy patch Faiz said I was becoming too touchy and persistent and assertive. Couldn't let go of anything that I couldn't control. One moment tough, over-sensitive the next. Like the man you're not able to be, I'd lob back. So much for my feminism. And then we'd be off again. But it's better now for sure since we've rearranged everything. Relentlessness. Repetition. Tenacity. I saw the writer jot that in her notebook, and something else about optimism that I couldn't read upside down.

I don't feel heroic or admirable. I feel stressed. If I allow myself to get too emotionally involved in each case I won't be able to do my job, I'll be no good to any of my clients. I manage by not taking it all on. I concentrate on what I'm doing. I try to be focused and supportive with the clients without giving false encouragement. These are vulnerable, marginalised people, often traumatised, with little idea of their rights, often filled with hope that everything will work out. They're susceptible to racketeers who pinch their money in exchange for promising to deliver their dreams. The Tory war on equal access to justice is killing us. When I started out, Legal Aid ensured that for a relatively low cost the whole system functioned. Now Mr. Gove is suggesting that equitable access to justice should be a charitable endeavour subsidised by philanthropy. Perhaps he'd like to bring back the poorhouses as well.

I want to share the rest of the wine with Faiz. Hear about his course and get him to rub my feet. But we're still hunting the Snark.

> 'For the Snark's a peculiar creature, that won't
> Be caught in a commonplace way.
> Do all that you know, and try all that you don't:
> Not a chance must be wasted to-day!
>
> 'For England expects – I forbear to proceed:
> 'Tis a maxim tremendous, but trite:
> And you'd best be unpacking the things that you need
> To rig yourselves out for the fight.'

The writer asked me what I wear for hearings. For judicial reviews in the High Court, where I'd be getting someone out on interim relief or a bail application, full wig and gown. Although I have done emergency ones, mostly hunger strikers in the detention centres, in shorts and t-shirt and Fitflops at a services station on the phone. I did one from Disneyland in a sarong, and another standing in a corner during a wedding. In the Tribunal I just wear a suit.

We'd talked about my worst war stories and all the grim stuff and by the time the coffee arrived risked sliding into dejection. She said enough already, tell me about the days you win. What it feels like. How you celebrate.

The best times are when a client is produced in the hearing and I can have a quick chat afterwards. Those are such precious moments. Sometimes I get to walk out of the building with them which feels pretty spectacular. But it often takes a while to get them out. If there's an electronic monitoring condition it can take a day or two.

First thing out the door it's always bands and wig off, then immediately ring the solicitor. If it's in the afternoon and I can get away with it I drag someone from chambers into the pub. Then usually about an hour, slightly less, after the exhilaration comes the crashing exhaustion. It's like walking out of an exam where you know you've got what you needed. Happy – then suddenly drained. Still happy – but either unable to concentrate on what's being said by whoever you're talking to or, like now, sprawled on the couch in dozy relaxed limbo. But starting to fret about tomorrow. I want to talk with my sweetheart about something blissfully hopeful, like grocery shopping or planning holidays. I just don't want to constantly bring the conversation back to what was said in the hearing.

The Sprout tickles my nose.

'Bedtime, or the court will issue you with a BABO.'

'What's a BABO?'

'Bedtime Avoidance Behavioural Order.'

'I'll go if you tell me exactly where the Snark lives.'

She's a shy child, but will never give up a point. So I make

something up with a bit of a Lewis Carroll letter I read
somewhere, and a tad of me.

> An island frequented by the Jubjub and Bandersnatch,
> No doubt the very island where the Jabberwock was slain,
> This place where you've landed,
> And we all want leave to remain.

The Voluntary Returner's Tale

as told to

Caroline Bergvall

I'M A STRONG MAN.
Even for me this is too much.
I'm so tired enough is enough.
15 years of this.
15 years without knowing.
15 years if I can stay if I can start a life.
15 years neither here nor home.
15 years of corridors and doors and hours and years of
   working my case and hoping and waiting.
15 years of corridors and doors and years of hoping.
15 years of paperwork and casework and English and flawless
   prejudice.
15 years of compiling files speaking to solicitors going to
   court working my case reading the decision.
15 years of corridors and doors and hours and years of
   starting again.
15 years of working my appeal going to court reading the
   reports being moved again.
15 years of being moved and being moved. Another appeal
   another report.
15 years I work my case this judge rejects it. From service to
   service court to court city to city.
I work my case that judge rejects it.

It's so hard. I've tried for so long. What you've been doing to
   me here it's not human it's not right.

waiting waits for ground
waiting erodes all ground
waiting loses ground
waiting steals all ground

So tired.

I was a student at a technical college.
I was studying for a commercial diploma just finishing my
   first year.
The terrible war had ended. The combatants had taken refuge
   in my country.
It all turned to chaos and violence.
Soldiers occupied the campus. They started killing we were
   scared.
There was trouble I had nothing to do with it. Except that I
   was there.
I went into hiding in the monastery.
2 years later the priest guided me across. I boarded a plane
   and felt safe.
I didn't know until then what asylum means.

15 years never knowing.
Always trying always hoping.
Working my papers working my cases.
Twice they've changed the flag in my country since I've been
   here.
Twice they've changed the name of my country.
15 years.

So tired.

On landing at Heathrow I went to the toilet.

When I came out of it I was the only one left at customs.
There was only one officer.
So unlucky.
He mistreated me mistook me for someone else kept on
    saying I was someone else.
Made me strip for no reason. Called me terrible things.
He put a really bad stamp on my application form.
I didn't know. I couldn't read my form in English.

But later I went to college and I learnt to read English.
I was educated to work hard. My father was a teacher.
He died when I was 10. I'm the only boy among 8 siblings.
At first we kept in touch. Now we've lost contact.

I'm here yet I'm not.
You'll never know.
That I was here.
Nor that I still am.

12 years ago in June I was refused asylum.
The immigration officers were not present at my hearing.
12 years ago the judge rejected my application for asylum.
I didn't know until I could read English how the officer at
    entry had killed my case.
So much hate on that form. Yet it's always been his word
    against mine.
12 years ago all support stopped.
I lost everything.
12 years ago everything college bus passes lodgings food
    vouchers. Everything just stopped.
Now I'm no longer an asylum seeker. Now I'm a destitute.

Still I needed to sign in monthly. It's 21 miles away.
How can I travel how can I find food I'm not allowed to work.
I need clothes need food need to get bus tickets just to be
    able to sign in.

How can I cope. I have to work I have to survive.
I should be long gone
yet I'm still here.
I can't leave
yet I'm not allowed to stay.

having arrived
might never arrive
having landed
will never land

'*Slow violence is neither spectacular nor instantaneous, but instead incremental, whose calamitous repercussions are postponed for years or decades or centuries. Emphasising the temporal dispersion of slow violence can change the way we perceive and respond to a variety of social crises. We are accustomed to conceiving violence as immediate and explosive, as erupting into instant, concentrated visibility.*'

One Christmas it's stupid I wanted to get my step-boy a gift.
     I took on a packing job.
Driving back with friends that night we were stopped by
     police.
So stupid.
Yes I'm guilty yes I'm destitute yes I was working illegally.
At the station the police were kind and reassuring.
But the day of my hearing it was snowing so hard that we
     couldn't get to the courthouse.
It counted as a no-show.
3 months on remand.
My case finally came up.
Lots of people had said you'll get 6 months. If the judge is
     bad you'll get 6 months.
He gave me 16 months.
I cried I can't anymore enough is enough.
Such a small mistake.

'Borders, it's not just where they stop but at what they stop what they enforce what kind of separation they enforce and what powers lie behind who sinks who swims who gets pushed under or pushed along. What measures and agreements are the deciding factors what internal and external policies, clauses and sub-clauses decide on who comes in and how and when and why and for how long how many stamps seals of approval times dates identity papers timelines checks and regulations will anyone need to sojourn within the invisible yet undeniably proliferating walls of this state.'

16 months!
That's immediate deportation.
Now I'm no longer a refugee no longer an asylum seeker no
    longer a destitute.
Now I'm a criminal.

So tired.

At the end of my sentence immigration came.
They took me to the detention centre.
It's a really long journey an 8 hours' drive.
When we reached the door I took one look.
Oh my God I thought I had served my time.

This is worse than prison.
Prison was tough but detention is the worst.
You're just there. No-one knows you.
Wake up nothing to do. Wake up eat sleep wait.
In prison there's the calendar.
Everyday you cross out a day.
Everyday one less to cross.
One less of waiting one more for hope.

Detention is the worst. A week is like a year.
I talk to someone who's been here one year.
And others who've been here 2 3 4 years.

What are they doing here.
I know I'm here for 2 weeks maximum.
They say you never know.
When they come for you.
And if you'll be deported or released.

I feel despair.
I'm a strong and patient African man.
This is not right what you do here.
It's not human what you subject me to here.

waiting eats the soul
waiting eats the bones
waiting eats the heart
waiting eats all hope

The Home Office declared an amnesty.
As they do from time to time to clear the backlog of cases.
I had a partner while in detention. But I was refused bail and
    couldn't travel to our joint hearing.
Where is your partner they asked and threatened her and her
    boy with deportation.
She got scared. They granted them indefinite leave to remain.
Now all my friends have paperwork.
Indefinite Leave to Remain. And they have families. And
    friends. And places to stay.

I have a son at home
he was one when I left
and a stepboy here
I can be a father to neither of them.

'Far from flattening the world and reducing the significance of borders,
the contemporary social regime of capital has multiplied borders and the
rights they differentially allocate across populations.'

In detention there's no access to solicitors.
But I'm a fighter. I will fight my own case.
Everyday I wake up with my file and go to the library.
10 months later my case comes up.
The judge takes one look at my file. And throws out my case.
Then he tells me
you're a danger to society.
Something broke inside me then.

'We must ask serious questions about the kinds of distinction that are being drawn between an 'economic migrant' and an 'asylum seeker,' or between someone with papers and someone without them, as these identities are increasingly formalised but also plagued by ever greater incoherence.'

I want to leave what's the difference.
Being killed here or there. Better to die at home.
My God I'm tired.
5 years ago I said enough. Let me go back.

The private security escort picked me up at the detention centre.
We drove in silence to the tarmac of Terminal 3. The van
      stopped.
I thought kill me here. I can go nowhere. Just kill me here.
No-one in the van moved. These people. Where is your
      decision my God.
I'm tired. If you say I can go let me go.
The van turned around and took me back.
Now there's one more fight in me!
I compile and fight a new case.
It leads to nothing.
Then another case.
Again nothing.

'Slow violence makes powerless steadily incrementally, a pervasive yet elusive form of bureaucratic abuse.'

How can it be.
In this country.
Treated in this way.

Just let me go back I'm crushed I can't do it.
No longer now I'm too tired no more no more.
Still they're not letting me go.
Still they're not letting me stay.
15 years I've been in limbo.
You want to deport me?
I want to go back!

*'Who do you suppose would dare to throw you out, Sir? said the
mayor to K... No one is keeping you here, but that doesn't mean
you're being thrown out.'*

3 years ago I applied for AVRR.
Assisted Voluntary Return and Reintegration.

*'Voluntary return – the orderly and humane return and reintegration
of migrants who are unable or unwilling to remain in host countries
and wish to return voluntarily to their countries of origin.'*

Why am I still here?

*'The successful implementation of AVRR programmes requires the
cooperation and participation of a broad range of actors, including the
migrants, civil society and the governments in both host countries and
countries of origin.'*

Why am I still here?

With a criminal record you can't get help to leave.
I need to return without assistance.
Assisted voluntary return is dangerous.
But unassisted voluntary return is only for the truly desperate.

Without assistance I cannot travel I receive no cash I get no
    help to buy my tickets.
I receive no protection and support no help with
    reintegration.
Returning without assistance most likely I'll be arrested.
I'll be mistaken for one of the combatants that are being
    trained over here.
Most likely I'll be confused for someone I'm not.
Who are you?
Why were you there?
What were you doing there all this time?
Why are you coming home?
Why have you come back?
I could be imprisoned and tortured I could die.
Whatever happens happens. Better die at home than
    continuing on like this.
This is not a life. It's just making me sick. I've tried so hard so
    long. Enough is enough.

I'm told. Go to the embassy.
I can't go to the embassy.
The embassy doesn't take in asylum seekers.
And the embassy doesn't deal with citizens who have a
    criminal record.

My case worker calls everywhere without getting through.

*'Borders, are they drawn at a natural obstacle, at a temporary political
boundary, at a set of shared language or languages, at preferred cultural
or class or caste types, in a far more widespread and sinister way at
preferred ethnic types, how far into a body do they reach, how far into
a person do they go to keep them out, with what impeccably argued
arguments is this person not worthy, not harmonisable enough, since
that's what it's called: harmonisation.'*

For a while they put a tag on my ankle.
My God. Why.
I fight the case.
They remove the tag.

This mental torture it's worse than a killing.
No longer no more no more.
I've been crushed nothing left.
15 years.
Enough is enough.
Better to die at home better to go quickly now.

I see people go to work live their life.
There's been another appeal.
I no longer want to know.
Just let me go.
God I'm tired.

'Migration has been defined in terms of a crisis that needs to be managed. The importance of migration in the contemporary world will not diminish.

One in 33 people in the world is on the move.'

The Support Workers' Tale

as told to

Josh Cohen

TRY THE DANISH, GO ON.

Ha.

We're not Mother Theresa or anything.

We laugh a lot.

Footballer haircuts, word-of-mouth tutors, high-end kitchen appliances, all that. Not so much piety, penance, prophetic rage, moral superiority.

The apricot ones are better.

★

So this young guy, 27 years old and *handsome*, tells me he'll never get a girlfriend. I say, 'You?!' because, you know, he *is* handsome, 'But why not?' 'Why not?! Where would we go? I can't even buy her a coffee.'

All the pain and humiliation. The money you don't have for a coffee you can't buy in a place you can't go with a girlfriend you won't meet.

★

We're all volunteers: teachers students social workers office managers physiotherapists software engineers doctors yoga teachers…

★

So when we talk about destitute asylum seekers, what does that really mean? Well, the obvious to start with – money, food, shelter.

But it goes beyond material deprivation, down to the destitution of the whole self.

It means being *in* but not *of* the world. Like a shade from the world below, you're condemned to float around outside, looking in on everything you can't have, everyone that you're not.

If no one sells you a pint of milk, or nods good morning or smiles or banters or flirts or asks you directions or if you want to come for a drink, who are you? If in the daytime you wander the streets with no place to go and at night you tiptoe across the floor of some dank, one-bed apartment and spread yourself across a battered sofa pretending not to hear the hissed altercations of your friend, or friend's friend, and his wife, about you being there?

Try to imagine it. You'd wonder if you existed at all, while feeling you exist too much, like there's no space to accommodate the burden of you.

★

We open our doors for three hours, first Sunday of the month.

As their numbers have swelled, so have ours. Close to 400 of them, maybe 100 of us.

We reimburse travel, yeah.

Somehow they get here, from a few or a few hundred miles away, however they can. Last time it took five buses for one man. Once he got here, he waited an hour for the doors to open in the blazing heat. Then he helped hand out drinks.

They get home-cooked food, shopping vouchers, clothing, medical attention, legal advice, counselling.

And they get us, and each other.

We welcome them, yes, but I always feel they welcome us too.

It's hard to explain.

★

Some people arrive morose and, well, leave morose. It's a mire of desolation.

And yet.

Such an uplifting place to be.

★

You look around the room, brimming with people, with all shades of colour and feeling and expression and age and you just think, stories.

★

Occasionally a client gets leave to remain, and then he'll come back as one of us. That's amazing. It closes the gap, lets us feel our basic sameness. Actually, just being here does that.

You look over at a loose circle of people in the middle of the room, sipping coffee, chatting. The older white people could be fleeing blood feuds in Albania or ethnic conflicts in Georgia, the younger black people could be volunteers from Croydon or Southgate.

We have an ex-client, he's a doctor. 90 years old.

We welcome them. They welcome us.

★

… Sunday leaguers choristers Minecrafters bloggers watercolourists kitchen gardeners…

★

It's hard not to be in awe sometimes. This one bloke has been coming for ten years, and every time I call to him, 'Hey, how are things!' 'Still alive!' he says, waving and smiling. Every time, 'Still alive!'

★

The resilience, the sheer tenacity of their hold on their humanity. You can't help thinking you'd have lost it long before, not knowing if tomorrow brings redemption, damnation or just the familiar grind of boredom and fear. Which is itself damnation, I tend to think.

★

You don't want to get sentimental. You get these bruisers come along, you've put out strawberries for the kids and they swoop down like bloody gannets, and before you can say 'hey!', they're gone, them and the strawberries both. Well, that's humanity too. You have to remind yourself: the most fundamental human right of all is probably the right to be as much an arse as anyone else. Let's not peddle the cliché that suffering makes you good. Or bad, for that matter.

★

A depressed baby.
Does it sound ridiculous that I didn't even realise there could be such a thing?

★

Goodness knows I'm no longer young, but I've been working with refugees since I was.
Decades.
In all that time I've not known a service like this one.

Living so many years outside the moneyed economy has the most bizarre consequences. This man, Gabriel, I'd known for years, I'd been helping him with his application, his evidence, trying to get him a little money. I came to find him where he was living, if you can call it living, in Northampton, to bring him down here, have him stay at my home for a while. His hostel turfed him out all day, so he spent his waking hours walking the streets, aimless and penniless.

Well! He insisted on taking me round all the places and people who'd shown him some kindness – the mental health centre, the local pharmacy… the William Hill! 'Yes,' he said to me, we had to go in the William Hill, and well, you can't help wondering why on earth a penniless asylum seeker feels he urgently needs to go into a William Hill. The answer was Marge. He had to see Marge, to thank her for all she'd done for him.

'What did she do for you?' I asked him. As he started to tell me, his eyes welled up. 'If there's not many people, Marge lets us come in where it's warm, maybe watch the racing. Sometimes you have to use the toilet, she unlocks the special toilet for us.' Think what that means, if you have no regular access to a toilet. So in we go, he asks for Marge and out she comes and he hands her this rather grotty bunch of flowers we've bought for her and starts to tell her all she's done for him, only he can't because by now the tears are flowing too thick and too fast. So there we are, this great big man, his arm suspended in mid-air, his tongue frozen in his open mouth, and this little Marge, well now Marge loses it, stares at these dowdy, cellophane-wrapped chrysanthemums and then at him and says, 'You're leaving us!' and then she's off too, weeping uncontrollably, and then of course it's my turn, the floodgates open and there we are the three of us, sobbing in chorus while behind us a little band of irritable men with three-day beards stare at the ground and tap their feet, waiting to put their tenner on the 3.30 at Aintree.

★

... Catholics Sikhs C of E Hindus Muslims Buddhists Jews Humanists Methodists New Agers...

★

The look on a little girl's face when you show her six pairs of gloves and invite her to choose the one she likes best.

When I saw that face, I thought, no, that's not a look of gratitude. It's a look of welcome.

You see?

★

It's a synagogue project, yes.

I was telling someone about it once. 'So what, are they all Jews?', he asked me. So I said yes, the majority of volunteers are Jewish. But he meant the refugees!

The refugees. From Sri Lanka, Congo, Eritrea, Iran, Bangladesh, Egypt. Seriously! 'Are they all Jews?'

You have to laugh.

★

One guy who comes here had spent three years in detention, then they released him. They can release you as abruptly and as arbitrarily as they arrest you.

You imagine if your life has been so malnourished, so bereft of everything that'd make it a life, you'd grab the chances that come to you with both hands and both feet.

Doesn't always work like that. Once he got bail, he had no clue what to do outside detention. Freedom was a kind of agoraphobic nightmare, the world spread around him like an unnavigable desert.

He struggled with addiction. And then it's a few steps to crime and then, well.

★

Yes, the founding group are Jewish.

The camps, *Kindertransport*, DP, just words, but more than words.

The ghosts of our early lives.

We went to school, we ate well, our parents worked hard and made sure we did too. And then round the table, amid all the daily laughter and madness, you felt the presence of the dead.

Faces suddenly turned inward, and sad. You felt it.

Sometimes I look at a man or woman here chatting or smiling, and there's a pause and I see the same gesture. The same gentle downward turn of the neck, eyes, mouth, the gaze fixed below as though that's where the truth is.

★

It's amazing, the way the four corners of the earth can fold in on themselves in here.

We had a Professor client once, from Rwanda. He comes in for a new client interview, and as he sits down there's this little gasp from the man interviewing him, a lawyer. The Professor, he tells me mouth and eyes agape, was his teacher in Kigali.

So he agrees there and then to represent him, *pro bono*.

★

If they want to talk about their stories, they will. You make yourself available to it.

But it's probably better not to ask. You get the feeling they've come to forget about their stories, just be ordinary.

The kids especially. You do something like firing elastic bands in the air, something as ordinary as that, and they're in ecstasies. They've never seen that before, they make you do it again. And again. And again.

★

A young man I'd worked with got leave to remain. I hadn't heard from him in three or four years, so when he phoned there was, I confess, a long pause before I could place him. He was going to college, he told me, could he name me as his next of kin? Me, who hadn't remembered who he was. That'll tell you something about destitution.

★

And then you can be destitute in knowledge.

A young woman, barely eighteen, arrives here pregnant and alone. Back home she'd have slotted into a family support network. Abandoned to herself, she's nothing to fall back on, not the barest bones of know-how. She has an emergency c-section, and then she's left with this baby. And questions. Why the bleeding? How do you care for this wound? How do you hold a baby?

How do you hold a baby?

★

Occasional fights break out in the kids' section.

No one's taught them what sharing is. And in any case they've not really had anything to share.

And then magically they do.

And you tell them they have to give it back.

★

… quiet young funny cantankerous odd kind shy overbearing morose elderly intellectual sporty needy daft generous…

★

Maybe the worst thing of all is the sheer brittleness of any life they can cobble together.

I've known people get the right to work, an NI number, some exhausting, low-paid, low-status work no one else wants to do, and gradually they put up some kind of scaffolding of a life.

Then, all of a sudden and for no real reason, the Home Office writes and says they've found your file, you've no right to work here, go home, you don't have a well-founded fear of persecution.

Fill in the wrong form. Make the wrong payment.

Some bureaucratic error, a technicality that suddenly becomes a crime. And the life you thought you had pops like a bubble.

★

The things you hear.

In churches, advice centres, doctors' offices, benefit offices.

'Give me a lethal injection please. I no longer want to live.'

'Someone tried to kill me with a knife when I was sleeping beside the shop entrance. That is just what I deserve.'

★

The kids who volunteer don't generally want to at first.

Well, yeah. Obviously.

Afternoon with the wretched of the earth. A real hot ticket.

They want to imagine their brand consciousness and gadgetry and expensive haircut is just part of the air they breathe, not the marks of their privilege.

So I got my kids to play with the kids here.

They have a great home and their own rooms and ridiculous amounts of stuff and good schooling and friends and leisure and hobbies and security and permanence and love, all abundant, all unquestioned.

But as long as they're playing, any differences between my kids and any other kids can stop mattering.

We can't give them all the things they need to live.

But we can give them the feeling of being alive. For the few hours they're here, but for longer too, because it's something they can keep hold of till they return.

★

... so they come from all over by foot by bus the backseat of a car of a friend of a friend they come weary hopeful sad smiling pissed off ravenous cold hot they come the fleshly beings they can now be assume the singularity of this life this body flabby old thin muscled weedy whatever body queuing as separate bodies hanging loosely together not dissolved into some snaking queue of postered hate they come to eat inside outside to know themselves as storied seen heard felt laughing with laughed at a presence in the world a foot you can step on a trunk you can bump into and have to say sorry laugh it off no problem to choose shoes you like because brown red because sole lights flash look FLASH! soul lights they come to eat as more than clamouring belly to eat dahl lasagne strawberries sticky sweet pastries or not because you don't like them they come to be recognised in law as minds as conduits for flow of blood desire feelings good bad to talk listen talk listen to be silent to feel the bare fact of another's presence of others' presence of own presence of being there taking up a rightful corner of the world they come to see their children play laugh strop be more than their needs your guilt they come and we come and we open doors and they open doors and we welcome them and they welcome us and feel the solidarity of the flow of blood desire feelings good bad to feel not love but something simpler the being-together of neighbours in a room in the world welcome and welcoming because this is the human race and there's only one whatever they come not to be loved but to be as we come not to be loved but to be to welcome them as they welcome us because there is no them and no us.

★

There are worse ways to spend a Sunday afternoon.
   I'd avoid the raisin ones if I were you.

The Soldier's Tale

as told to
Neel Mukherjee

WHAT DO WE WANT from the world? It's a question that crops up again and again in my head as I process the applications and read the case files and the histories they contain. They are histories of the worst in us. Or maybe I need to refine that: they belong within a spectrum where the term 'worst', as the superlative form of 'bad', simply does not apply; an overused, ordinary word such as 'bad' or 'worst' holds no meaning here. I leave it to you to imagine what is done to, say, two ten-year-old girls seized by a rabble of male soldiers of the Lord's Resistance Army. And this is my guess: you won't be able even to cross the threshold of the unimaginable, let alone begin to get anywhere near what actually happens. Which body parts to bend and buckle and twist, which to tear, rip, slash, gouge, which to burn, with fire or acid... the creativity on this is boundless, leaving the imagination exposed as such an old-fashioned tool, an abacus in Silicon Valley. I read pages and pages of these every day. Sometimes just a bare mention of an atrocity, without any details, is the most troubling, leaving me to imagine the lacunae and, then, I do not know which is worse – the imagination succeeding or failing. But still I read them, I *have to* read them, because I am a cog in the wheel of the giant machine that determines whether these torn, branded, gassed, fleeing people can make a new life for themselves in a new country where they are safe from harm.

Such a small thing to want from life, don't you think, to be safe from harm?

But you learn very quickly that you have to turn down most of them. What you also learn is that gradually the human mind begins to insulate itself in the face of such evidence – or narrative, if you will – to the point that you start to protect yourself from what you read. You have to. Nice twist, isn't it, that they come to you seeking protection and you end up protecting yourself from them?

There's nothing in Salim's application that is extraordinary or atrocious or eye-catching. In fact, exactly the opposite – the commonest argument made is that the applicant will be killed/tortured/imprisoned if he is sent back to the place he has escaped from, and this is the centrepiece of Salim's too. He is from Asmara in Eritrea and at the age of seventeen or eighteen he is forcibly conscripted by the army in 1996 and sent off to fight in the Eritrean-Ethiopian War that begins in 1998. He is told by the commander in charge that his military service is going to last for a mere six months. The six months prove to be elastic. After six years of being moved from camp to camp, fighting against Ethiopia, against Djibouti, Salim summons enough courage to confront his commander about this broken promise, for which Salim is first detained, then confined in an underground prison. The prison houses nearly 400 men and twenty of them, Salim among them, dig their way to escape after one year. Soldiers fire on them and while the narrative is not forthcoming on how many the soldiers got, Salim survives and after walking for one month, he enters Sudan illegally, without any papers.

Salim is in Sudan for eight years, and the record of his time there is sketchy, especially given the crucial things that occur – a marriage to an Ethiopian woman called Abeda (a Christian who works as a cleaner), the birth of a son, family trouble issuing from the fact that Abeda has married not only an Eritrean, the national of an enemy state, but, insult to injury, a Muslim, leading, eventually, to Abeda returning to Ethiopia, leaving the child in the care of Salim's mother, who travels to Sudan to look after him. The account of the time in Sudan is perfunctory, and skates so quickly over such important turning points that my suspicions, honed by years of Home Office training, cannot help but be aroused.

These are the things that we've been trained to winkle out of applications and use to demolish the arguments for refugee status. The more you read the more you notice that sometimes the arithmetic is not quite accurate: the date of birth changes, the number of years on the run, or in hiding, or moving from one place to another can be variable, the accounts contradictory or inconsistent here and there, things not adding up properly. And yet something in Salim's application gets through. Sometimes, even for the hardest of apparatchiks, a detail catches hold...

Whatever the reality of the matter, or the accuracy of the finer details, two salient points emerge from the Sudan chapter. The first: Salim works – illegally, in the black economy – in Sudan for the eight years he is there and saves enough money to pay US$1000 to a trafficker, Omar, to go to Libya, where he is promised a regular job, a better life, papers. The second: a son he leaves behind with his mother. This latter fact belongs to a category we call 'discretionary', the unsaid rule being that it is, or should be, orthogonal to any decision made about the refugee's leave to remain.

Salim belongs to a group of thirty men who are driven, each tied to a big truck, for four days until they arrive at a border town where they are sold to rich Libyan men. It is here that Salim realises what the racket is: slavery. The Libyan man, Ahmad, who buys Salim, takes him to the desert to look after sheep. Salim joins a group of eight such 'shepherds', all of them housed in a bunker in the middle of nowhere. He works here for six months without any pay; there's nowhere to escape – he is in the middle of the Sahara. The hard calculation that leads Ahmad to return Salim to Omar, the racketeer boss, after six months remains opaque to Salim but when he asks Omar for money for all the labour in the desert, Ali says that there's no money for him and if he dares to ask again, he will kill Salim himself, or have him killed by his goons. There is nothing for it, so Salim travels to Benghazi and from here to Tripoli, where he stays for a year, working odd jobs, in construction, as a handyman, lifting, carrying, and saves up enough money to pay a further US$1600 to yet another trafficker who promises him and 84 others – 60 men and 25 women – a new life, a better life, a decent working life in the paradise across the waters that is Europe. Yet again Salim falls for it – what can be worse than this life as an illegal low-grade labourer in an alien city? Better to cross the Mediterranean to life in the wealthy North, the land of hope, of jobs.

What do we want from the world? A point of rest, security, the tacit assurance that one will be able to live the full trajectory of one's life, from birth to death, without any shock denting or cutting short that arc. More, perhaps: a home, enough to eat, freedom from illness and disease and the capacity to get treatment for them when they afflict us.

The inflatable dinghy is 11 metres long. 85 humans are packed onto it. The traffickers point out the cylinders of fuel, then pick two men to drive the boat and show them how to operate the engine and push the dinghy into the waters. It is the dead of night. A few hours into the sea, the passengers discover that the dinghy has holes in its bottom. For one day and one night, they take turns bailing water out of the boat until the engine sputters and stalls in international waters. They bob and float, bailing water, on the vast open sea for four days. Then they are spotted by a Tunisian fishing trawler. The fishermen cannot repair the dinghy's bust engine but what they are able to do is call the Italian police, who arrive in a helicopter, then a big ship, which saves all 85 of the refugees.

They are taken to Lampedusa where they are fingerprinted. This is an important moment, both an arrival and the beginning of a kind of imprisonment, but Salim doesn't know this yet. The new life is new but not in any way he has imagined. He will find out. The new arrivals are taken to the refugee camp near Catania. Fifteen months elapse as Salim's application is processed by the Italian authorities. At the end of this period, he gets his five-year *soggiorno* and is released from the camp into the freedom of Italy. The new life begins.

He has no money, no home, no job, no benefits, no Italian, nothing. For nine months he sleeps on the streets, eats from garbage bins, sifts through rubbish heaps for clothes, a stray dog among humans. He is sick, frequently. He moves from city to city, from Catania to Palermo, Rome, Messina, begging, foraging, homeless, until he fetches up at Milan and manages to board a train to Calais and join the 'jungle'. He loses his Italian documents and phone in a 'jungle' portaloo and reports the fact to Calais police. For the twenty days that he is there in the 'jungle', he tries to jump each day onto a Eurostar – on the open truck carrier of the train – headed to London. One day in July he gets lucky – he manages to give everyone the slip, hide under a truck on the Eurostar and come to Dover. He immediately seeks asylum at the border. After two months at Dover, the Home Office decides – I mean *we* decide – to deport him back to Italy: under Section 4 of the Immigration Act, he is eligible for refugee status only in the European country where he first disembarked and was fingerprinted, which is Italy, and not allowed to 'shop around'.

Salim refuses 'very strongly' to board the flight and is taken to an immigration removal centre near the airport. Every few days, the Home Office cancels and reissues tickets to Italy and he is carted off to the airport and even on to a plane. On one occasion, the pilot refuses to fly with a forcible deportation case on board his flight. In detention, Salim is visited by someone from a visitor's group. (In a rare aside in the application, Salim notes, 'Without them I would have killed myself. They took me from dark to light.') Then in accordance with new rules about moving refugee applicants to different parts of the country, Salim is relocated to Glasgow. He has to report in person to the local Home Office outpost every two weeks. At any of those visits, he is liable to be detained and removed to Italy. He is still suspended in this purgatory, waiting and hoping and dreading. One could diminish a man to nothing, to chaff, to dust, with this; the only weapon you need is time.

And the reason Salim doesn't want to be returned to Italy? Quite apart from the life of a street dog he had there, there is this line in his application that stands out: 'I cannot see the difference between Eritrea and Europe – I'm not free in any of those places.' And this is what pierces through my hard shell. That line. And then those lacunae again: what do they use to bail water entering the dinghy through the holes? What do they talk about when the engine dies in the deep sea? How does he save $1000 in eight years in Sudan or, more importantly, $1600 *in one year* in Libya? How does he hear of the traffickers, of a better life in Europe? Who tells him these things, who convinces him? What goes through his head as he tries to smuggle himself into a Eurostar every day for twenty days and is caught every single time? How many attempts does he give himself? After which attempt does he think, 'Enough, I'm never going to make it'? Does his mother send him pictures of his son as he grows up? What is the one-month walk from Eritrea to Sudan like? What does he eat during that time? How does he travel between towns and cities in Sudan and Libya? What is the network of people keeping him alive, allowing him a toehold in the black economy in foreign, unknown countries? Why does he say that he would rather kill himself than go back to Italy? What is it like to arrive in a new world and find it to be exactly the same in substance and soul and impossibility as the old? And then, you see, once the questions press, the formal application is nothing; the story that is alive, the person that is alive in the story, lies in the answers to the hundreds of questions I want to ask at every turn. I want to know, to imagine, every single detail: from the food he eats in the shepherds' hut in the middle of the Sahara, the exact nature of what looking after sheep entails, to how much money he makes a day on average begging in the streets of Italian towns, what he and his compatriots used to dig out of the underground prison in Eritrea. Thirteen years in different kinds of confinement or on the run escaping from them, trying to find some measure of freedom, and failing each time, with every turn of the story, a seemingly eternal repetition of the pendulum swing between hope and the crushing of the hope.

Another small thing to want from life, don't you think, to be free? And yet it is everything, not only to them, but to us, too, who they hope will save them.

And what does the world want from the people in search of a point of rest? Nothing.

The Mother's Tale

as told to

Marina Warner

THE SACRISTAN OF THE CHURCH of Our Lady of Sorrows in a suburb of Northwest London was chipping at the wax deposits from the candles on the stand in the side chapel where the special miraculous statue looks down from a starry conch, glinting blue and gold mosaics. She was a small wiry woman, in her seventies, I reckoned, and I went over to her to talk – since the recent ferocious sentences on the Gatwick Fifteen, who tied themselves to the undercarriage of a plane in protest, and the murders of the MP Jo Cox in Birstall and the Pole Arcadiusz (Arek) Jozwik in Harlow, and the battering of the teenager Reker Ahmed in Hounslow, my editor's been telling me to follow up on refugee stories. I'd heard about the case of Cecilia Onyegupo and her family, at high risk of deportation. They were regular attenders of services and dos at the church, so I was hoping to be given a way of meeting them.

The sacristan told me her name, Dympna, when I showed her my business card. She knew the paper I work for – the local free rag, door to door – and she was happy to talk:

'I first saw Cecilia after Mass – oh, it must be several years ago – and I noticed her because, well, she isn't someone you'd miss, would you? Even now, after everything that's happened to her, she's still one of those people you could say God lavished with gifts – you know, when he made us in the

Garden of Eden. Father Damian says, and he has a way with words, that we were truly beautiful, then. Like leopards and gazelles, roses and oranges, pools and streams, and the angels were overcome by the beauty of it all, when they first saw creation, they spread their rainbow wings wide and waved them up and down, to show God they appreciated his work, that's what Father says. We have stained-glass windows here of the days of creation and the artist − a woman who lived nearby, Gwen Tindley − made them in the 1950s when the church was built; she shows Adam and Eve and the gorgeous blossoming trees and flowers and shrubs in Eden. I think she went to Kew Gardens to research them − my Dad knew her because he worked in Maintenance of the Parks and so on for Camden and she was local too and used to wander around.'

The sacristan was well embarked on telling me how she was now a Londoner, written all the way through the rock, but her father had been part of the huge wave of Irish who came over in the Sixties to find work in England; he'd worked for Camden Council for decades and when he passed away, she said, she and her five sisters gave him the full send off, four black horses with black ostrich plumes drawing a glass carriage through the streets with his coffin inside completely covered in flowers, one of the wreaths in the shape of a tankard of Guinness and another a darts board.

'I do the flowers for the altar, too, so I know a bit about that side of things. We have tours coming here to see the church, as it's a fine example of modern architecture. The Twentieth Century Society was here just the other day and they were full of admiration… and they were very surprised we have such a flock here, but we do.

'We flourish. People come here from everywhere. We are a big family.'

'And Cecilia Onyegupo?' I put in. I had to bring her back to the subject. 'And Ambrose Ilofu, her partner? My editor's keen to get human interest stories − about people like them, so we see they're human after all, could be you and me…'

Dympna stopped flaking the wax from the metal stand and her mouth quivered, 'We're praying for Cecilia – and for the children and for her husband… we know Ambrose isn't her husband, not properly, because of their situation and their documents. Or rather their lack of documents. The church isn't allowed to marry them, not when they're "illegals". We've been able to baptise the little girls, Francesca and Madeleine, that's a mercy. Father Damian would like to be able to – marry them, Cecilia and Ambrose, to each other, I mean – Ambrose is such a good man, she is such a good woman, such a handsome couple, both of them so faithful. Father Damian's *sore afflicted*, that's the honest truth of it, about the whole situation. The law prevents him. But I know, he knows, and they know, I hope, that in the eyes of Our Lady and Our Lord they are husband and wife, I feel sure they are. Our Lady is merciful towards sinners.' She glanced across at the statue.

'People don't like to know this, but Africans are the pillars of our community. Many, many members of our congregation come from Nigeria, so I know them well, and how they are, how they look, from different parts of the country. It's a huge country. Cecilia is an Igbo from near the huge city of Onitsha and you can tell, they all have something, the women especially. Ambrose is Edo, that's Benin country. Really you can't imagine what a wonderful lot of people they are. She is typical – but also exceptional.

'It's a crying shame what's happening to her – and to many others. A waste, a crying waste.'

She went back to tackling the deposits with a penknife, tipping them into a pail on the floor, so much residue of years, the wax permeated with whispered entreaties as the candles caught alight:

– Dear Mary please make Bobby Diamond notice me and ask me out.

– Dear Mother Mary please make my period come – I am two weeks late and I never meant to do it.

– Blessed Mother Mary please help my little boy to recover.

- Blessed Mother Mary Our Lady of Sorrows help me pass my GCSE in Maths.

I dropped a fifty pence coin in the padlocked metal box on the wall and drawing out a candle from the sheaf, touched it to the burning wick of one on the rack. I don't believe in such things, really, but under my breath I entreated the Blessed Virgin just the same, for something, anything, to set things right, somehow.

When Dympna'd manicured the candle stand to her satisfaction, she wandered off to the steps of the high altar, and began clipping dead flower heads off the arrangements in the vases, me trailing behind her with my tape recorder.

'The little girls are very dear – Maddie'll be making her first communion next year, all being well - DV, as Father says. If... if... if...' she lowered her voice and looked around the church theatrically, 'You never know where the UK Border Force – name courtesy of our current Prime Minister when she was Home Secretary – where the UK Border Force's eager beavers might be lurking.'

She crossed herself and looked over at the statue of the Blessed Virgin. 'Sometimes I think I will catch her moving, you know,' she whispered to me. 'If I move my head quickly enough, she'll be smiling at the baby and adjusting him in her arms, and nodding in agreement that she's going to act, she's going to do something about the state of the world, and all this.'

The sacristy door opened and a pudgy middle-aged man in shirtsleeves waved at Dympna and came across the gleaming floor towards us walking through the coloured pools of light falling from the stained glass, as the April sunshine pierced it with boiled-sweet brightness.

'Father,' said Dympna. 'This lady's from the local paper. She's after inquiring into Cecilia and Ambrose...'

'Yes?' He had peaked eyebrows and their points sharpened.

'We're campaigning,' I explained, 'against Indefinite Detention and other legal abuses of our democratic traditions of justice.'

'Ah, that's good,' Father Damian nodded at me. 'For a moment, I thought… you know how things are, then.'

He paused and closed his eyes slowly then re-opened them, as if hoping the scene before them would have changed. 'I am seriously thinking of offering Sanctuary here,' he went on, 'in our church. As in churches in times gone by.

'I don't think Our Lord would be happy with the language we are hearing these days, the threats people are facing. Only the other day, in Kentish Town, my counterpart the parish priest there, Father Xavier, tells me that a well-known local citizen, friendly with everyone who came in the health food shop where he worked, where he had been working for 14 years, who had lived in this country making no trouble for nearly three decades… that is *three zero* years… after he fled the violence and civil unrest and prejudice in the former Yugoslavia, this person was taken away in the early hours, told he was going to be sent back home. Home! Somewhere that does not exist any longer. His country's disappeared from the map… where's he to go?

'This is how the Romans behaved to the Christians – at first. This is how Saul conducted himself before the road to Damascus and the great light blasted some sense into him and he became Paul.

'This is like… I shan't say, but what echoes do you catch in the sentence that the Prime Minister spoke a few years ago when she was Home Secretary? She said then – to the *Daily Telegraph*, not your paper – "The aim is to create here in Britain *a really hostile environment* for illegal immigration." What does that mean? It means sweeping up all kinds of people, branding them with the same stigma regardless of their contribution, their humanity. Think of the echoes. It's chilling, don't you think?

'And she the daughter of a vicar! Anglican, mind you, but still, I don't think the Archbishop – this one or the last one – would find that sentiment very creditable, do you?

'I am a man of peaceable habits, isn't that so, Dympna? But I am going to ask Our Lady or perhaps St Dominic to provide.

A big brass door knocker that nobody wants any longer, that's what we need. I'm then screwing it into our front door so that a decent loving couple like Cecilia and Ambrose can enter here and find sanctuary – if the worst comes to the worst.'

He was shaking his head and his cheeks had spots of pink under the badly shaven white stubble – must be saving on his razor, I noted, or have a badly lit shaving mirror, and it made me feel he must be sincere.

Dympna said, 'That's all very fine, Father, and I am sure Our Blessed Lady will grant your prayers, but for the moment Cecilia and Ambrose need practical help.

'There are Maddie and Frankie to think of, too.

'Ambrose has been taken away – *detention*, they call it – three times,' she went on. 'Each time indefinitely. Each time, nobody knew if he would be coming back to the family. But he has, so far. Still the threat remains. It's very hard on Cecilia. She takes it very hard. She's nothing like the young woman she was when she first started coming to church here.'

Through Dympna and Father Damian, I managed to arrange to go round and see the family. They are living in a single room, about a third of the size of a tube carriage. Cecilia was sitting on the sofa looking wan, as she was ill and had been in hospital.

'The nurses were so gentle with me…,' she said, wonderingly. 'They asked me so kindly whether this hurt or could I feel this…' She was astonished to be treated with sensitivity, with respect. 'I think,' she said, 'I would like to go to school and train to be a nurse.'

Ambrose explained that this room was bigger than the first one the family lived in. It was very full of furniture, with a three-piece suite which opened into their beds, and a fridge, a telly, and a wardrobe. The kitchen was off the hall and, like the bathroom, shared with other tenants in the building. The hall space was crowded with plastic bags. The lights were kept down, to save on electricity.

Cecilia said she first saw Ambrose during Mass, but it was at the jumble sale afterwards that they began chatting. He was studying at Middlesex University to be an engineer, specialising in gas pipeline technology and computer programming. It was a Sunday in spring, Mothering Sunday seven years ago, and Father Damian had preached about Moses' wife. Moses' family didn't like her, because she was a foreigner. When she had a little boy, and then another, the children were in danger too from hostile feelings around them.

They began chatting, she said. 'And Ambrose was so friendly.' She was smiling when she spoke his name and I could see, in the soft light that came into her eyes that, in spite of her exhaustion and her anxiety, that slim handsome young man in the clean, ironed shirt and crisp trousers who had a degree in engineering and was paying such attention to her.

'We began seeing each other…' she sighed and her voice slowed, 'Then the first baby – that's Maddie, well, she arrived.'

Ambrose added, 'I was working for a company, I was a computer engineer. But I overstayed my visa. For six years now, I have been an "illegal immigrant".' He repeated what Dympna had told me: he'd been picked up three times, taken to a detention centre. 'And every time they didn't tell me how long I'd be there, or if I would be allowed to stay here in the country, or if they would never see me again, Cecilia and the children.'

The little girls were wearing little boots and tights with patterns, and dresses with flowers on the fabric, and they had their hair braided round their heads with one or two beads on the tufts. They were very keen to tell me how they had been in the Nativity play at Christmas, the little one had been cast as a lamb in the shepherds' flock, while the elder one, Maddie, had been given a proper part, the Angel Gabriel.

'She has a big voice,' said her mother, 'for a chit of a girl.' During the hymns she sang out very loudly:

> 'Then sings my soul
> My saviour god to thee

How great thou art
How great thou art.'

She smiled and laughed, quietly remembering. Frankie, the younger one, went on, 'I had cotton wool and white crepe paper all over my head and body like snow. There was a bit of snow, not then but later, and when we played in it it was soft but then it was wet. Mum made my costume but it was difficult to keep on. She tied it to my arms with shoelaces out of my trainers that are too small.'

'I really like the hymn,' said Maddie:

'Then sings my soul
My saviour god to thee
How great thou art
How great thou art.'

They clasped one another and danced about in the space between the sofa-beds in the room.

Cecilia was saying, 'We don't need much of anything. I do the children's hair and I would like to work at something like that... hairdressing, yes, perhaps – if I can't train to be a nurse. But we aren't allowed to work, you know that.

'And I am afraid,' she went on. 'I am so afraid. Although Ambrose hasn't been taken away again, not for several months now, I am still afraid it will happen – any time.'

Ambrose spoke to her, soothingly. 'It is a process. We have to go through the process. We have to be patient. When Maddie turns seven we can make an appeal again to stay.'

The reading from the Bible that day, during the Mass when Ambrose and Cecilia met, was from the second chapter of the Book of Exodus. Dympna was the reader. It was the passage about how Moses is a stranger in a strange land because he was living in Egypt and later, had to flee from there too. To Midian, the stretch of territory between Egypt and the Holy

Land which is now called the Sinai... a kind of no man's land. There Moses married. His wife was called Sephora and like Moses she too was a foreigner in Egypt, and she became the mother of his boys, Gershom and Eliezer... 'And Ger in Gershom means,' Father Damian was saying later during the sermon that day, 'a sojourner – a passing stranger... a stranger in a strange land.'

The pink spots on Father Damian's cheeks were very bright and the stained-glass lozenges falling from the windows were bathing the pulpit and the paved nave in front of him, in rays of emerald and scarlet, and he kept reassuring them that Mary is the Mother of Mercy and that human beings are filled with compassion. He had been a choirboy and was still a good singer and when he intoned the call for responses and spread his arms for the blessing like archangel's wings, he seemed to stretch out to hug everyone there. He could make you shiver through and through.

'You, my dear parishioners,' he told them from the pulpit, 'so many of you, here in our family at the church of Our Lady of Sorrows, you too are strangers in a strange land. And Moses and Sephora and their babies foretoken what is to come when Mary and Joseph and the baby flee into Egypt from Herod and his murderous rampage. Like so many of you again who have had to flee your countries and your rulers' crimes.

'Moses understood what it is not to be at home: he was left in the bulrushes and he could have died... then when he grew up he had to take flight again, because of an incident – a violent incident – and he was involved, though it is likely he was provoked. But anyhow on this day, a day dedicated to all mothers everywhere, we must remember how his mother took a job as his nursemaid, all unbeknownst to Pharaoh's daughter who had rescued Moses from the bulrushes and taken him to her palace to raise him as her own.

'And let's not forget – on this day dedicated to all mothers – the story of Sephora, who was the wife of Moses when he grew up. She too was from another country, a strange country.

She was a Midianite, somewhere from the country between the Holy Land and Egypt.

'She was black. Or perhaps she was brown.'

Later, Ambrose began sitting beside her during Mass, Cecilia says, but she remembers that on the Sunday they first met, he turned to look at her where she was sitting behind him, while Father Damian was talking about Sephora.

Ambrose's father was the first in the family to convert to the Catholic church. When the missionaries arrived, he was suspicious: white men before came to take not give. But one of them gave him a bicycle so he could go to the secondary school which was farther away in the town. Ambrose laughs. 'The missionaries built a school for us, too, and a hospital, planted all around with mango trees. Beautiful.'

Cecilia is telling me quietly what a good man Ambrose is, how he provides for her needs, and that her needs and the little girls' are not very many, but he finds what she likes and brings her fruits that are the same as fruits from home. She shows me: a pair of small round gourds with dimpled rinds. Mangosteens. They haven't eaten them, perhaps they are too rare a connection with the past.

That Sunday seven years ago, Cecilia was tuning in and out to Father Damian as he preached to his flock, so many of them strangers and more frightened now than they were then to go out in the streets, where only last week an asylum seeker who, when asked who he was, said that he was an asylum seeker, and was savagely beaten up.

Ambrose tells me, 'When people learn we are "illegal immigrants", they change their attitude towards us.'

Cecilia tells me, 'I am so afraid to go out.'

She does not go out, not any more on her own. Ambrose always does the shopping and he takes the little girls to school and fetches them.

'Sephora was black. Or perhaps she was brown. She might have been an Arab or an African, like so many of you,' said Father Damian. 'Moses married her because her father was grateful to him for helping his daughters water their cattle – they had been set upon by locals who were angry they were there, using their well.

'Moses sprang to their defence.

'For this good deed, Jethro – for that was the name of Sephora's father – gave the young stranger his Sephora for a bride.

'But Sephora also became a stranger when she married Moses, who was a stranger in a strange land himself.'

Father Damian, preaching his sermon for Mothering Sunday, was flushed and almost had tears starting down his cheeks as he trained his burning eyes on the crowded church where so many of his flock were arrivants – some of them asylum seekers, some of them immigrants of long standing. His lovely voice rumbled and rolled through them.

When the girls were at school Cecilia would listen to the services on television. She didn't sing along because she couldn't, she said, but she liked remembering her little girls, especially Maddie, giving voice:

> 'Then sings my soul
> My saviour god to thee
> How great thou art
> How great thou art…'

When they were home, their springing about added a spring to her spirits, too.

She would forget, briefly, to be afraid.

She wanted to remember things to tell them about when she was young.

But her mind was filled with fear. Fear slid down her mind's eye like a blind against sunlight and shut everything off.

'My mother used to tell me stories,' she told me, 'but I don't remember anything. All I can think of is what might happen. How he might be taken again and sent back. How I would never see him again.'

The little girls were dancing about, trying to catch her attention to tell her about their day at school, how it had been Hand-Washing Day. They skipped about and laughed as they showed her,

> 'This is the way we wash our hands
> Wash our hands
> Wash our hands
> Wash our hands…
> Splish splash splosh
> Splish splash splosh!'

'Mummy is always very, very strict with us,' they were saying, 'about washing our hands when we use the toilet, because there are many other people in the same house with us and they are not very friendly. Mummy and Daddy keep the toilet clean for us but they are sometimes cross about it, and it makes Mummy sometimes sad, too.'

The little girl wrinkled her nose. Then they both skipped over and hid behind the sofa and began whispering, playing houses and hushing imaginary babies.

Cecilia is trying to remember a song her mother sang, which she used to know when she was her children's age. But she can't.

'I am afraid,' she says, 'all the time. It's all I can think of. And when I try to remember, my mind's a blank.'

The Smuggled Person's Tale

as told to

Jackie Kay

AND HE HAD TRAVELLED some distance before he arrived at the house. He'd come all the way from the seventh area; he'd come from the Hazara people, Afghanistan. He'd a bad time in Turkey, had caught a boat to Greece, crossed the border to Italy, spent months in Rome. He'd slept under bridges, in train stations, under berths of trains, in the back of lorries. Austria, France. Calais – Christmas 2009. Cold. Very cold. Big snow. The road was near what they called the Jungle. He'd travelled for seven years and crossed countless borders. He'd taken on different names, and had often said he was from Pakistan. You could measure the distance in the look that crossed his face as he crossed the threshold into her house.

Moments before he'd been lost: the street had two houses with the same number at opposite ends. He had been down the other end. It was nothing to him compared to all his journeying, but still when he first arrived, with his story in his rucksack, he was out of breath. He was sweating a little. Tiny beads formed across his forehead. His eyes first searched hers for kindness. It was the thing he always looked for; he could tell right away if people were kind or not. She opened the front door. It was a simple enough thing for her – to open the front door to her home. But to him it was quite something. Over these years of travelling, he'd not often been invited into many homes. Detention rooms, prison cells, hostels, on the floor of various churches, yes, but he'd not been invited into people's houses. He stood in the hall as she went to make a pot of tea. He stood there with Anna, who was already there when he got there, who was the only person in the world who knew what he carried in his bag. Both he and Anna stood quietly, patiently, in the hall, waiting. Only this time the waiting was nice waiting; this was waiting for something quite simple: a cup of tea.

When she finished making the pot of tea, she walked from the kitchen to the hall with two steaming mugs in her hands. She was surprised to find them still there. A little embarrassed. Make yourself at home, please, come in come in, she said, rushing. She'd expected that they would just go into the living room and sit down. But they'd waited to be polite. As if they had both learnt not to make any assumptions about anything, or to take anything for granted. It made her pause in her own hall and think of all the things she took for granted. The list was already starting to grow in her head.

And he sat down in her small living room. And he looked around with some excitement. Here he was - G. He was in a house in Chorlton, Manchester, England. The UK. He had made it to the UK. He was safe, he thought. And so was his story. He had it in his green rucksack. He had smuggled it in.

The woman was ready to take it. He sat down to get it out of his bag, confidently. He was shocked to find it wasn't there. He emptied everything out, in a mild panic. It'd been in there when he was on the bus; he'd checked. He pulled everything out. Half a sandwich, a pen, some official papers. But his story had gone. His eyes darted from side to side. He started to sweat a little more. It must have fallen out, he said, like my phone the time I was hanging on to the lorry, when the roads hurtled past with terrible speed. I heard my phone splinter and crash and then I heard something run over it. It had everything in it and then was gone. He shrugged his shoulders to indicate that he was used to losing things. He had lost his country, his children, his wife, his farm. The days when he used to farm wheat in Afghanistan were over.

It was a strange thing. He had lost all the big things there were to lose in life. He'd witnessed the death of many friends – one friend had been shot, another had fallen from the underbelly of the lorry. (You didn't have a chance when travelling at that speed. His friend just lost his grip and the road took him.) Another had disappeared. He had no idea where his mother or father were. He had no way of contacting them. He had lost everything there was to lose and so it was the small things that got to him, that made him nearly tip over, that made him flip. The mobile phone. The photograph. The small key. One journey had blended with the other. Once, he'd tried to smuggle himself across a border, under the belly of the lorry, and he hadn't made it and had been arrested. It was strange, that time. He had gone to the bathroom in the police station and had not recognised his own face. He was another man in the mirror. The soot covered everything. His face, his hands, black. Totally black. It made him gasp. It startled him, his own strange reflection. There was already something of himself that he did not recognise because parts seemed to be falling off. Perhaps they were left on the road too. He laughed out loud at himself in the mirror. It was a shock. And he felt shy to be so filthy. When he came out of the toilet they let him have a shower. They said don't worry everyone that comes here from under the lorries is that colour. And they gave him clean clothes. He hadn't expected that. Along the way, sometimes, on life's strange and hard journey, small acts of kindness took his breath away and made his chest hurt. His eyes regularly filled with gratitude, shining and dark.

When he came to her house, J's, and she opened her door, and her face was all smiles, he thought he still had it in his bag. The story was in the bag, he could have sworn it! He couldn't believe what had happened after all the miles and the countries and the crossings, all the borders and hidings, all the smuggled nights and hidden mornings of hunger, thirst and fear, that now it should suddenly be lost. They sat quietly in the room with all the nice things, and they waited, all three. It was as if they all shared the same breath. Time slowed right down. Time passed in an easy way for him. It was neither the fraught waiting time of detention or the terrifying waiting time of clinging onto a lorry's low-slung belly. It was waiting like a tree might wait for blossom.

And it was then that he heard something under the room that all three were sat in. A kind of beating noise. The house, her house, was over a hundred years old, she'd said earlier. Under this room was a cellar. It had no natural daylight, J said. He got up from the living room. He heard himself saying, is it OK? and J nodded, though for the first time that day she looked uncertain. Alone, he crept down the steep stone steps and wove his way through piles of empty suitcases and brimming full black plastic bags, old paint pots and brushes, step ladders, boxes of books and papers, and right in the corner, huddled under the fuse box, was his story. He had no idea how it had got there.

He picked it up. It was an injured bird. Its heart beating like its wings used to beat. He held it gently and cooed to it, stroking the feathers in the same direction. He didn't want to frighten it. He was full of wonder. How did you get out of my bag and change into a bird he asked his story? He was shaking. But it wasn't the same shaking that he'd felt in the prison, or in the detention room, or in the back of the police car, or hidden under the sleeping berth of a train, or holding onto the lorry's underbelly, or locked in the boot of a car to make a getaway. Of all the shaking, he had done in his life, this shaking was very different. He found to his complete surprise that he was trembling with joy.

He called for J to come down. He still didn't feel it was quite right to call her by her name, as she didn't feel right to call him by his either. So he shouted, 'Hello!' It was a word that could do for everybody. 'Hello!' But she didn't come down. She said a funny and shocking thing. She said she was frightened of her cellar. She came to the top of the stone steps and said, 'I can't come down. I'm frightened.' He said, 'I've found it.' She said, 'Bring it up,' and she disappeared from the top of the stone stairs. 'Goodness me,' he thought, 'how strange.' She wouldn't even linger there; she didn't even like looking down into it, her cellar. A space like this was vast to him compared to the tight spots he'd been crammed in on his journeys. Should anyone have ever offered him a cellar such as this, he would have been more than happy! He picked his way through the lines of disinfectant, dishwasher, polish, and toilet cleaner, paint stripper and old brushes and gently carried his injured bird up the steep steps. He felt as if a time had passed between arriving there lost and finding the trembling bird. It was difficult to keep his balance and not drop the injured bird, who clearly already had put its full trust in him and searched his eyes with its own dark beady eyes. It loved him already. Birds form quick devotions, he thought in his own tongue because he couldn't find the words for that in English.

When he got to the top of the stairs, he came straight into her kitchen where she'd been making the tea earlier. The kitchen door was open. It was a very sunny day. Can you imagine? After the freezing snow on the journey from Calais, after all the rains and ice and frost, crazily cold in the wrong clothes, here he was suddenly hot in sunny Manchester? And he had just found his story, which had changed into a bird with a broken wing.

Look, he said. Here it is. And he started to tell J all the time cradling the bird, holding its beating heart to his own. He started with the weather. The big snow he had been through, the slow traffic in the lorries from Calais. He told her of all the winds and the rains and the snows and the heat. Of the borders he had crossed. Of all the places he had hidden. Once he had hidden amongst all the canisters. Once he had hidden where he was sure he would be seen, and he had not been seen, yet his friend had been seen, and the driver had told the immigration officer there were two of them in there. Yet he had not been found that time. It was strange. It was like magic.

Like he'd found the power to be invisible. Like he was his own card trick. A human card. Somebody called him that one day. You're a card. It made him laugh. A lot of the things that had happened to him, to be honest, were funny. Laugh out loud hilarious. When he told people his story it made them gasp and roar in equal measure. They said to him, you really did that? They were astonished. That time with the canisters, it seemed he was even able to hide from himself. The man had been in there with his flashlight and had just not seen him. He was excited, thinking back to this, how he'd just got away with it that time, how he'd managed to vanish. Or maybe the man had seen him and decided to let him go. Just him. Like a single fish, back to the water.

He thought of how he had been treated in his own country, how the Hazara people were treated, how he never felt safe. In fact, no matter how dangerous these journeys had been, no matter how many crossings, nothing compared to the fear he had felt amongst the people who ruled his country. They would just shoot you. One time in the boot of a car, he was sure they would all be shot. The first layer of his skin had been ripped off in his own country. It is the worst thing in the world – when your own country suddenly doesn't feel like your own. When you are cast out from within. When you are made a foreigner on your very own soil. It started to flow. One journey jumbled with the other. The bird trembled in his hands. It is OK, he told his story. It is OK. Out it came, bit by bit, chunk by chunk. He could feel himself lighten. His feet were barely touching J's red tiled kitchen floor. He was embarrassed by everything he had lost in his life. But a smile kept catching the corners of his mouth. He couldn't help it. That last crossing when he made it against the odds, after many, many attempts, even the police had started to say *you again* when he arrived back at the police station, that last time was something. Even the police had started to pity him in certain places. He was a man on the run from the country, his own country, that was not safe for him anymore. A smile kept breaking like the early light in the sky, and something actually shifted. It was a mysterious thing. Life.

He looked into the eyes of the beautiful brown bird. He didn't know its name. A thrush. It was a song thrush without a song. He was its song. He considered the bird's dark, dark eyes. They were like onyx or jet, moist and deep as the soul of a river. And perhaps because he felt welcome, he could at last take his time. He sat down at the kitchen table still holding the bird. He held it out to J. Take it, hold it for me a little while so that I can drink a glass of this cold water and eat a piece of this bread. She took it. He found out later that she was also scared of birds. She had carried it to her back door. And perhaps because the door was already open, it flew through it, a strange lopsided flight, one-winged, but full of hope, and made it to the slate roof across the back of the terraced houses, and then to a shared chimney, and then paused, as if to say, look up here, look at me, here's your story. And then, astonished, he watched it take to the sky; perhaps it crossed the River Mersey and perhaps after that it would cross many other rivers, many rivers to cross, before it landed, perhaps back home. Or maybe it was on a day trip somewhere to Blackpool, or the Lake District, or further north to Scotland or further again to Shetland. He didn't know where it would travel to anymore. It wasn't his anymore. He got out the letters and the certificates, the pieces of paper that had once caused him utter shame and embarrassment, which had once made him frightened just to look at his number and his name, which had once made him tremble, just the letter head, just the words Home Office. He left them on the table for her. He would be elated if he never had to look at those types of papers ever again, never had the dread of one of those letters clattering through the letterbox.

For now, he could leave it behind. And so he did. He left with his bag beautifully light after months and years of carrying the weight around with him. He stepped back into the street. Still sunny. He waved goodbye. He promised he would one day return. And then he was gone. Into the still warm day, into the yellow spill of light, into the great good of the day, when welcome was all that was in his head now, and the rest of the terror for the moment had lifted. What a feeling it was. What a city, Manchester! How kind the brothers.

One day, like a carrier pigeon, his story might return with a new message in its mouth.

Anna left with him. She was smiling too, smiling like a modest midwife. She was the one person who had helped smuggle his story into the world. Her voice was light and quiet. For months in the dark windowless detention centre, that voice had been his lifeline. Every Wednesday, she came to visit, and brought him food. He hadn't known how to explain that part. It was like she helped him too much, he said, widening his arms. My heart expanded, he'd said. And now, it was something, wasn't it something, to be able to walk together, out of the house and up the street, the street with the red brick houses and the slate roofs, the terraced street with shared chimneys, the birds lined along the rooftops, to walk with Anna along this quiet street, side by side.

Afterword

Calling for an End to Indefinite Detention

The Walk

As THE SUBTITLE OF the project has it, *Refugee Tales* is A Walk in Solidarity with Refugees, Asylum Seekers and Detainees. Originated in 2014 by the Gatwick Detainees Welfare Group, as a response to the silence that surrounded indefinite immigration detention in the UK, the project first walked in 2015, from Dover to Crawley via Canterbury. Following the route of the North Downs Way, that inaugural walk was framed by the location of detention centres: the Dover Immigration Removal Centre (since closed) situated on Dover's iconic White Cliffs, and the Brook House and Tinsley House Immigration Removal Centres at Gatwick Airport. In 2016 the project walked again, from Canterbury to Westminster, via Dartford. This year, 2017, we walk to Westminster from Runnymede, site of the signing of Magna Carta. The purpose of the walk, straightforwardly, is to call for an immediate end to indefinite detention, the UK being the only country in Europe that indefinitely detains people who have sought asylum. The way the project makes that call is by telling stories; giving public performances everywhere we stop. Modelled on *The Canterbury Tales*, *Refugee Tales* sets out to communicate the experiences of people who have sought asylum in the UK, and who, having done so, find themselves indefinitely detained.

With each new walk and with each new series of tales, so the political landscape through which we are moving has altered. When Refugee Tales first walked, in June 2015, it was just after that year's general election, but just before the intensification of the crises of displacement that saw refugees compelled towards Europe on an unprecedented scale. In 2016 the project walked in the immediate aftermath of Brexit, but also after the passage through parliament of the Immigration Act. As we walk this year it is after the election of Donald Trump, but, more pressingly in this context, after his attempted ban on travel to the United States from certain Muslim countries, one immediate effect of which has been an increased use of arbitrary detention.

Refugee Tales' objective has not altered; we continue to call for an immediate end to the UK's policy of indefinite detention. What has changed, however, is the prominence of detention as a political concern. As regimes around the world – Australia, Hungary, Turkey, the USA – make the news through the ease, frequency and cruelty with which they detain, so detention appears increasingly and alarmingly to be a defining issue of the present time. To detain a person indefinitely is fundamentally to breach their human rights. To call for the practice to end is to draw an ever more necessary line.

Making its way across southern England, through villages and suburbs to central London, the Refugee Tales walk is one way of establishing that line. People who have been detained and whose movement post-detention is variously micro-managed and intimately obstructed – whether by electronic tag, exclusions from public transport, or periodic 'dispersal' from one part of the country to another – walk with people whose movement and residency is not under threat. Participation is sometimes compromised by bail conditions, in that people who have been released from detention on bail have to report their continued presence in the UK to the Home Office. If they don't report they might be re-detained; re-detention is always a threat. What the walk enables, even so, is the circulation of stories. Not just the Tales but the stories that come up constantly in conversation as the walk takes place – it being just such circulation, of people and stories, that UK immigration legislation appears determined to prevent.

Real as the walk is, and acutely real as are the experiences presented in the tales, there is a significant sense in which *Refugee Tales* is also symbolic. What it aims to do, as it crosses the landscape, is to open up a space; a space in which the stories of people who have been detained can be told and heard in a respectful manner. It is out of such a space, as the project imagines, that new forms of language and solidarity can emerge. What *Refugee Tales* counters, in other words, as it calls for a change of policy and language, is what the authors of the immigration act have called a hostile environment.

The Hostile Environment

For all the shifts and ruptures that have characterised politics over the past two years, the development that has most closely impacted on people detained indefinitely in the UK was a predictable one. On 12th May 2016 the UK government's new Immigration Bill made its final appearance in the House of Commons, the provisions of the Act coming into force in various stages from January of this year. Like the Corn Laws of 1815, or the Poor Laws of 1834, the Immigration Act of 2016 is a monumental piece of legislation, the kind by which, one day, historians of the future will read us.

When people arrive at that retrospective reading, one of the historical tensions they will observe is that, although its formulation and early passage through Parliament preceded it, in its later stages the Bill coincided with what the media has called the migrant crisis, but what we might term instead, to borrow a term from the Canadian poet Steve Collis, the crisis of displacement. Describing her intentions for the legislation in 2012, the then Home Secretary told the *Daily Telegraph* that, 'The aim is to create here in Britain a really hostile environment for illegal migration.' How, one might ask, is such an environment brought to pass?

In its final form, the 2016 Immigration Act runs to 228 pages and 96 provisions. It is thorough to the point of exhaustion in its attention to the ways the 'environment', 'here in Britain', has previously allowed for a certain degree of assistance to be given. So much so that, as they have come to register its implications, civil society groups, NGOs and lawyers working with people seeking asylum have wondered how, under the terms of the new act, it will be possible to continue to help. In its thoroughness the legislation is not easy to summarise, though one quite quickly gets the measure of its tone by the kind of new powers it introduces.

In Part 3, for example, titled 'Enforcement,' provisions 46-58 concern the new 'Powers of Immigration Officers'. The enhanced powers are various but what they largely detail are the permissions granted immigration officers to 'seize documents.' In particular that seizing can now take place without warrant in residential premises and the documents can be retained for longer periods.

Part 4 of the legislation addresses 'Appeals'. The changes here build on significant curtailments of rights to appeal introduced in the 2014 Immigration Act, but also significantly extend the concept of deport first appeal later. What this means is that many appeals involving human rights which could once have been made 'in country', in the UK, will now only be possible 'out of country', which is to say in the country to which the person has been removed. The effect of such a re-locating of the appeals process is that the individual's prospects for success are significantly diminished.

Most immediately damaging are the new provisions in the area of the asylum seeker's rights to residence. Thus, whereas previously a person who had been released from immigration detention on bail was entitled to accommodation at the hands of the State (in light of the fact that they are not entitled to work), under the new legislation such accommodation will be increasingly (which is to say extremely) difficult to obtain. At the same time it is an offence for a landlord to enter a private rental agreement with a person whose status is unresolved. Between a rock and a hard place, the inevitable and already visible outcome of these changes is large-scale destitution, with local authorities only required to pick up the slack in cases of 'destitution plus'.

One area of immigration legislation goes unchanged, though its re-confirmation in the Bill is a statement of intent. Thus, in spite of a UNHCR report[1] expressing concern that in UK Removal Centres individuals may be detained for prolonged periods, and in spite of a cross-party parliamentary inquiry[2] into the practice that recommended the immediate establishment of a 28 day limit on immigration detention, and in spite of a late amendment in the House of Lords to the same effect, the new Bill confirms the Secretary of State's right to 'indefinitely detain' a person who:

a) has been sentenced to a term of imprisonment for a term of 12 months or longer; or
b) the Secretary of State has determined shall be deported.

To which three remarks should be added: first, that it is a most extraordinary area of legislation that would permit detention beyond the prescribed sentence; second, that the effect of the legislation as a whole is to so criminalise the asylum process as to make the commitment of a crime (for instance, trying to leave the country under false papers) so much more likely; and third, that a person can be 'determined' ready to be deported for years and years, well over a decade in some cases – though invariably, in such cases, deportation simply isn't possible, and though eventually, after years of waiting, the person may well secure leave to remain.

Indefinite immigration detention is, in theory, administrative: a person will be detained only pending 'removal' to their 'country of origin'. In practice, however, a person can be detained under UK immigration rules for months or years. As unbearably protracted as the detention itself can become, so the beginning of the process is disturbingly arbitrary. The early morning raid, as the first volume of *Refugee Tales* documented, is a tactic of choice. Once picked up the person detained will be taken direct to an Immigration Removal Centre, although the identity and location of the removal centre will often not be made clear.

From the moment of detention, two broad outcomes are possible. The first is 'removal'. The second is that the person will be 'released' back into 'the community', a process sometimes (but not always) triggered by the provision of bail. In 2015 (the most recent year for which Home Office statistics are available), over 50% of the 33,189 people detained were 'released' into the community, either because their appeal process hadn't ended or because it was not in practice possible (due to officially acknowledged levels of risk) to remove the person to their country of origin. And so the detention, whatever its duration, will not even have served its stated administrative purpose. It will however, as Lord Shaw's report to the Home Office on the Welfare in Detention of Vulnerable Persons[3] established (if it needed establishing), have proved traumatic.

Language

In ways that can only be guessed at in this Afterword, but in ways that the tales in the book make compellingly clear, indefinite detention is a profoundly traumatic experience. Clearly and principally, this is to say, detention damages individual lives. The causes of that damage are multiple and a full account of the situation would require contributions from many angles. In some senses, however, and by no means insignificantly, the damaging effects of detention and post-detention existence are visible at the level of language.

There are many ways to register this. It is a stark fact, for example, that hearings in the UK asylum system are not courts of record. What this means is that neither the bail hearings that might enable a person to be released from detention, nor the appeal hearings that determine whether or not a person will be deported, generate a written transcript. The latter will eventuate in a determination, being the judge's account of his or her findings, but there is no transcript, no complete record of the questions asked and the answers given. In the context of the asylum hearing (this is to say) the appellant's words are not recorded.

Where the exclusionary practice is most acute is as it bears on the currency. Thus, if a person is released from detention they are then entitled to subsistence-level support. Such support is necessary since, pending the resolution of their asylum case, they are not allowed to work – a circumstance (pending resolution) that can commonly continue for well over a decade. During that period the person is entitled to a payment of £35/week (£5/day), amounting to a level of poverty that when protracted is inhibiting on everything other than subsistence. Where the drive to exclusion manifests itself most clearly, however, is not in the amount but rather in the form of the payment, which is issued not in cash but in the form of vouchers. The vouchers take the form of a top-up card, an Azure Card so-called, that can only be spent in designated outlets, some of which (sometimes all of which) might be a long way from the person's house. It can also only be spent on designated products, the list of which involves notable exceptions; it can't, for instance, be spent on public transport. The total effect of such a payment system is that the currency itself goes untouched. Such un-touchability, it would seem, is hardly accidental.

There is a more general sense, less easy to capture in particular details, in which the person seeking asylum in the UK is locked out of the language. Thus, at every point at which the person who has sought asylum encounters the processes that constitute the system, what they encounter is an effort to thwart, disrupt, or discredit their account. Such discrediting takes all manner of forms, from the kinds of questions asked in official circumstances, to a refusal to accept basic facts of linguistic exchange; that, for instance, a person who has just fled persecution will not necessarily have a clear sense of how to communicate their experience, whether to a friend, or to an official, or even to themselves. At the level of official exchange, in other words, the experience that is decisive to a person's life is prevented from entering, or gaining access to, the language.

To put this more constitutionally, as contemporary UK culture defines itself by its legislation, what that legislation sanctions is repeated acts of silencing. This is all too familiar historically, of course; there has always been silencing. There is a difference, however, between knowing silencing to be an historic fact of the formation of culture, and standing by as such silencing forms and informs the culture one is a part of – where 'inform' functions a little like what the poet Gerard Manley Hopkins called 'inscape', the culture taking its character from the hollowness within. What one sees repeatedly, in other words, and with an intensity that increases year on year, is the fact that, in a way that simply isn't metaphorical, the language is the border. It isn't the whole of the border, nor its most manifest aspect, but it is absolutely a medium in which the border takes effect.

Due Process

In starting out from Runnymede, the 2017 Refugee Tales Walk (1st July to 5th July) begins at the site of the establishment of the rule of law. Two 'chapters' in Magna Carta set the tone:

> 39. No free man is to be arrested, or imprisoned, or disseised, or outlawed, or exiled, or in any way destroyed, nor will we go against him, nor will we send against him, save by the lawful judgement of his peers or by the law of the land.
>
> 40. To no one will we sell, to no one will we deny or delay, right to justice.

A person could, if they really wanted to, query the terms of Chapter 39. Who, one could ask, is the 'free man'? Who are his 'peers'? Any equivocation, however, is over-ruled by Chapter 40, where the universalising tone of Magna Carta is inscribed: no one is to be denied right to justice. What this combination of principles became is what modern law understands as 'due process', perhaps the clearest expression of which is to be found in the Constitution of the United States. As the Fifth Amendment puts it, no one shall be 'deprived of life, liberty or property without due process of law'.

The purpose of the Fifth Amendment is to provide protection: protection against the law by ensuring that the law itself respects the rights that are owed to the individual person. Such protection is intended to apply in all contexts, but in particular what it is designed to guard against is the arbitrary deprivation of liberty. Indefinite detention, in other words, is an offence against due process. And to be clear, what follows from such a breach is that the individual person is rendered absolutely vulnerable: subject to the law's immense power but without equal access to the law's protections.

No legal phrase is, in itself, ever a guarantee – witness the rapidly increased use of detention in the US since the election of Donald Trump. Technically, in fact, UK law is not bound by 'due process', in that the phrase itself has never been enshrined in statute. This is hardly to argue (as no democratic politician would be likely to argue) that in the UK 'due process' does not apply. As much as by any principle, in other words, it is by 'due process' that the UK would claim to hold itself to account. How could it not, since it is fundamental. 'To no one,' as Magna Carta stated, 'will we [...] deny [...] right to justice.' Or as Article 6 of the Universal Declaration of Human Rights put it in 1948: 'Everyone has the right to recognition everywhere as a person before the law.' From which it follows, as Article 9 of the Declaration necessarily asserted, that 'No one shall be subjected to arbitrary arrest, detention or exile.'

With Article 6 of the Universal Declaration of Human Rights the authors of the document arrived at a most important formulation. It is principally a legal formulation, of course, in that its purpose is to underwrite the application of law. It is also, however, a picturing of a better space; what the philosopher Hannah Arendt, writing in *The Human Condition*, would call the 'space of appearance'. What Arendt understood, in arriving at that phrase, was that when a regime seeks to refuse a person's recognition before the law, its first move is to prevent the person from making an appearance. This is what the Immigration Act of 2016 sets out to do; it sets out to stop people appearing. It is what indefinite detention seems designed to effect. Detention separates people out so that, in a literal sense, they are not recognised – so that the fundamental claim they have to due process is not allowed to become real.

What Refugee Tales sets out to help achieve is a space of recognition, a space in which stories that are routinely discredited, thwarted, disrupted and disbelieved can instead be safely heard. This can sound utopian perhaps, and in some contexts the first volume of *Refugee Tales* has been presented as utopian writing, which might be said to catch the spirit of the project, but also indicates just how far expectations have dropped. There is not, or at least shouldn't be, anything utopian about the demand that 'Everyone has the right to recognition everywhere as a person before the law.' Imagine the alternative. Such a demand is basic.

The larger context in which the stories that constitute *Refugee Tales* are told, the hostile environment, means that when it comes to publication anonymity has to be carefully observed. The stories presented here are the tales of people who have been detained indefinitely in the UK and who, pending resolution of their cases, are liable each time they report to the Home Office to be detained indefinitely again. For this reason, real as they are, the stories have to be anonymised and, as was described at length in the first volume, they are mediated by the writers to whom they have been told. This, it must be underlined, is only one of the project's methods of telling stories. During this year's walk, just as at the day-long forum with which last year's walk opened, people who have been detained tell their stories for themselves. The tales presented here, by contrast, are collaborations, between the person whose story it is and the writer with whom they were in conversation. The experiences presented are real, and part of that reality is the necessity of anonymity in publication. That they are collaborations, however, means that, in a significant sense, the stories presented in this volume have at least been shared.

To detain a person indefinitely is to breach the principles that underpin due process, a principle that has its origin in Magna Carta and that achieves forceful expression in the Universal Declaration of Human Rights. Those documents weren't for nothing. They were an attempt to stop cultures acting at their worst, to ensure that the power of the law is checked by due access to the law's protections. What they call for is the mutuality of recognition, a recognition which is rooted in the proper hearing of stories. In the present moment the stories of people who have been detained indefinitely demand to be heard.

David Herd
May 2017

Notes

1. UNHCR, Briefing Note, *Committee in Advance of the visit by the European Committee for the Prevention of Torture and Inhuman or Degrading Treatment or Punishment (CPT), Visit the United Kingdom 2012,* UNHCR London, August 2012; see http://www.unhcr.org/en-au/5756ec877.pdf, last viewed 18.6.2017.

2. *The Report of the inquiry into the Use of Immigration Detention in the United Kingdom: A Joint Inquiry by the All-Party Parliamentary Group on Refugees & the All-Party Parliamentary Group on Migration,* March 2015; see https://detentioninquiry.files.wordpress.com/2015/03/immigration-detention-inquiry-report.pdf, last viewed 18.6.2017.

3. *Review into the Welfare in Detention of Vulnerable Persons: A Report to the Home Office by Stephen Shaw,* January 2016; see https://www.gov.uk/government/uploads/system/uploads/attachment_data/file/490782/52532_Shaw_Review_Accessible.pdf, last viewed 18.6.2017.

About the Contributors

Caroline Bergvall was born in Germany to a Norwegian father and a French mother. Her work has been commissioned and shown by such institutions as MoMA, Tate Modern, and the Museum of Contemporary Arts in Antwerp. Her books of poetry and hybrid writing include *Strange Passage: A Choral Poem (1993)*, *Goan Atom (2001)*, *Fig (2005)*, *Alyson Singes (2008)*, *Meddle English (2010)* and *Drift* (2014). A former director of the writing programme at Dartington College, Bergvall has also taught at Cardiff University and Bard College. From 2007 to 2010, she was the Arts and Humanities Research Council Fellow in the Creative and Performing Arts at the University of Southampton. She is currently based in London.

Josh Cohen is a psychoanalyst in private practice, and Professor of Modern Literary Theory at Goldsmiths University of London. He is the author of *Spectacular Allegories (1998)*, *Interrupting Auschwitz (2003)* and *How to Read Freud (2005)*, as well as numerous reviews and articles on modern literature, philosophy and psychoanalysis, appearing regularly in the *TLS*, *Guardian* and *New Statesman*. His latest book, *The Private Life*, was published by Granta in 2013, and addresses our current raging anxieties about privacy through explorations in psychoanalysis, literature and contemporary life.

Ian Duhig (b. 1954) was the eighth of eleven children born to Irish parents with a liking for poetry. He has won the National Poetry Competition twice, and also the Forward Prize for Best

Poem; his collection, *The Lammas Hireling*, was the Poetry Book Society's Choice for Summer 2003, and was shortlisted for the T.S. Eliot Prize and Forward Prize for Best Collection. Chosen as a New Generation Poet in 1994, he has received Arts Council and Cholmondeley Awards, and has held various Royal Literary Fund fellowships at universities including Lancaster, Durham, Newcastle and his own alma mater, Leeds.

David Herd is a poet, critic, and teacher. He has given readings and lectures in Australia, Belgium, Canada, France, Poland, the USA and the UK, and his poems, essays and reviews have been widely published in magazines, journals and newspapers. His collections of poetry include *All Just* (Carcanet, 2012), *Outwith* (Bookthug, 2012), and *Through* (Carcanet 2016). His recent writings on the politics of human movement have appeared in the *Times Literary Supplement, Los Angeles Review of Books, Parallax* and *Almost Island*. He is Professor of Modern Literature at the University of Kent and a co-organiser of *Refugee Tales*.

Rachel Holmes is the author of *Eleanor Marx: A Life*, serialised on BBC Radio 4 Book of the Week and shortlisted for the James Tait Black Prize. Her previous books include *The Hottentot Venus: The life and death of Saartjie Baartman* and *The Secret Life of Dr James Barry*. Her most recent collective book projects include *Fifty Shades of Feminism* and *I Call Myself a Feminist*. Holmes is Visiting Literary Fellow at Mansfield College Oxford. Her biography of Sylvia Pankhurst is to be published by Bloomsbury in 2018.

Jackie Kay was born in Edinburgh in 1961 to a Scottish mother and a Nigerian father. She was adopted as a baby by a white Scottish couple, Helen and John Kay, and grew up in Glasgow. She studied English at the University of Stirling and her first book of poetry, the partially autobiographical *The Adoption Papers*, was published in 1991 and won the Saltire

Society Scottish First Book Award. Her other awards include the 1994 Somerset Maugham Award for *Other Lovers*, and the Guardian Fiction Prize for *Trumpet*. Kay writes extensively for stage, screen and for children. Her drama *The Lamplighter* is an exploration of the Atlantic slave trade. In 2010 she published *Red Dust Road*, an account of her search for her biological parents. Jackie Kay was appointed Member of the Order of the British Empire (MBE) on 17 June 2006. She was Professor of Creative Writing at Newcastle University, Cultural Fellow at Glasgow Caledonian University and is now Chancellor of the University of Salford, and Writer in Residence. In March 2016, it was announced that Kay would be taking up the position of Scots Makar (national poet of Scotland).

Olivia Laing is a writer and critic. She was born in 1977 and lives in Cambridge. She writes and reviews widely for the *Guardian, New Statesman, Observer* and *New York Times* among other publications. She's also a regular columnist for *Frieze*. Her first book, *To the River*, was published by Canongate in 2011 and was shortlisted for the Ondaatje Prize and the Dolman Travel Book of the Year. Her second book, *The Trip to Echo Spring*, about writers and alcoholism, was published by Canongate in 2013. It was shortlisted for the Costa Prize and the Gordon Burn Prize. Her new book, *The Lonely City: Adventures in the Art of Being Alone*, is in an investigation into loneliness by way of art. It was published by Canongate in March 2016.

An author, poet, illustrator, historian, and naturalist, **Helen Macdonald** is the author of three books, including the 2014 memoir *H is for Hawk* – which was a finalist for the National Book Critics Circle Award and won the Samuel Johnson Prize and the Costa Book Award. Macdonald describes the year spent training a notoriously difficult-to-tame species of raptor, a Northern Goshawk, as she mourned the unexpected death of her photographer father. Earlier books include a collection of poems, *Shaler's Fish*, and a cultural history, *Falcon*. An affiliated research scholar in Cambridge University's history and philosophy of science department, Macdonald writes and narrates radio programmes and appeared in the 2010 BBC documentary series *Birds Britannia*. She wrote the script for filmmaker Sarah Wood's *Murmuration x 10*, which premiered at the Brighton Festival in 2015, and recently completed filming a BBC/PBS documentary about goshawks wild and tamed.

Neel Mukherjee was born in India and has lived in the UK since 1992. His first novel, *A Life Apart (2010)*, won the Writers' Guild of Great Britain Award for best fiction, and his second novel, *The Lives of Others (2014)*, was shortlisted for the Man Booker Prize, the Costa best novel award, and won the Encore Award. His forthcoming novel, *A State of Freedom*, is out in September 2017. He divides his time between London and the USA.

Anna Pincus, a founder and co-ordinator of Refugee Tales, has worked for Gatwick Detainees Welfare Group for ten years, supporting people held in immigration detention and the volunteers who visit them weekly, managing outreach work and raising awareness about the campaign to end indefinite detention.

Alex Preston is an author and journalist. His first novel, *This Bleeding City*, was published by Faber & Faber in the UK, and across twelve further territories. It won the Spear's and Edinburgh Festival first book prizes as well as being chosen as one of Waterstones New Voices. His second book, *The Revelations*, was shortlisted for the *Guardian*'s Not the Booker Prize. His third, *In Love and War*, was published to critical acclaim in July 2014 and selected for BBC Radio 4's Book at Bedtime. Alex appears regularly on BBC Radio and television. He writes for *GQ*, *Harper's Bazaar* and *Town & Country Magazine* as well as for the *Observer*'s New Review. He teaches

Creative Writing at the University of Kent and regular *Guardian* Masterclasses.

Kamila Shamsie, novelist, was born in 1973 in Pakistan. Her first novel, *In the City by the Sea,* was shortlisted for the Mail on Sunday/John Llewellyn Rhys Prize, and her second, *Salt and Saffron,* won her a place on Orange's list of '21 Writers for the 21st Century'. In 1999 Kamila received the Prime Minister's Award for Literature in Pakistan. Her third novel, *Kartography (2004),* explores the strained relationship between soulmates Karim and Raheen, set against a backdrop of ethnic violence. Kamila Shamsie lives in London and Karachi. She has a BA in Creative Writing from Hamilton College in Clinton New York, where she has also taught Creative Writing, and a MFA from the University of Massachusetts, Amherst. She also writes for *The Guardian, The New Statesman, Index on Censorship* and *Prospect* magazine, and broadcasts on radio. She has written *Broken Verses* (2005), and *Burnt Shadows* (2009), an epic narrative which was shortlisted for the 2009 Orange Prize for Fiction.

Marina Warner is a writer of fiction and cultural history. Her books include *Alone of All Her Sex: The Myth and the Cult of the Virgin Mary* (1976), and *From the Beast to the Blonde: On Fairy Tales and their Tellers* (1994). The same year she gave the BBC Reith Lectures on the theme of *Six Myths of Our Time*. More recently she has published *Stranger Magic: Charmed States and The Arabian Nights* (2011) and *Once upon a Time: a Short History of Fairytale*. Her last novel, *The Leto Bundle* is about a refugee through time; her third collection of short stories, *Fly Away Home* was published in 2015. She is Professor of English and Creative Writing at Birkbeck College and a Fellow of All Souls College Oxford. She is currently working on the theme of sanctuary and a novel about her childhood in Egypt. She was awarded the Holberg Prize in the Arts and Humanities in 2015 and she chaired the judges panel for the Man Booker International Prize (2015).

Acknowledgements

The editors would like to thank everyone the Gatwick Detainees Welfare Group has worked with in detention, whose stories inspired Refugee Tales. Thank you to the writers and to those who shared their tales. Thank you to all the people involved in the planning of Refugee Tales including the Chairs of the committees, Mary and Christina, and John for website management and much more. Thanks to Katie, Avril, Marie, Mary, Dan and James, who have taken the book, and our message, to parliamentarians. Thank you to our patrons Ali Smith and Abdulrazak Gurnah. Thank you to the ICA, ThaiAngle, the GDWG and the University of Kent. Thank you Becca, Becky, Sarah and Ra at Comma Press for unending dedication to the project.

Refugee Tales
Volume I

Edited by Anna Pincus and David Herd

ISBN: 9781910974230
£9.99

'A wonderful way of re-humanising some of the most vulnerable and demonised people on the planet.' **Shami Chakrabarti**

Two unaccompanied children travel across the Mediterranean in an overcrowded boat that has been designed to only make it halfway across...

A 63-year-old man is woken one morning by border officers 'acting on a tip-off' and, despite having paid taxes for 28 years, is suddenly cast into the detention system with no obvious means of escape...

These are not fictions. Nor are they testimonies from some distant, brutal past, but the frighteningly common experiences of Europe's new underclass – its refugees. While those with 'citizenship' enjoy basic human rights (like the right not to be detained without charge for more than 14 days), people seeking asylum can be suspended for years in Kafka-esque uncertainty. Here, poets and novelists retell the stories of individuals who have direct experience of Britain's policy of indefinite immigration detention. Presenting their accounts anonymously, as modern day counterparts to the pilgrims' stories in Chaucer's *Canterbury Tales*, this book offers rare, intimate glimpses into otherwise untold suffering.

Featuring: *Patience Agbabi, Jade Amoli-Jackson, Chris Cleave, Stephen Collis, Inua Ellams, Abdulrazak Gurnah, David Herd, Marina Lewycka, Avaes Mohammad, Hubert Moore, Ali Smith, Dragan Todorovic, Carol Watts, and Michael Zand.*

Protest

Stories of Resistance

Edited by Ra Page

ISBN: 9781905583737
£14.99

Whatever happened to British protest?

For a nation that brought the world Chartism, the Suffragettes, the Tolpuddle Martyrs, and so many other grassroots social movements, Britain rarely celebrates its long, great tradition of people power.

In this timely and evocative collection, twenty authors have assembled to re-imagine key moments of British protest, from the Peasants' Revolt of 1381 to the anti-Iraq War demo of 2003. Written in close consultation with historians, sociologists and eyewitnesses – who also contribute afterwords – these stories follow fictional characters caught up in real-life struggles, offering a streetlevel perspective on the noble art of resistance.

In the age of fake news and post-truth politics this book fights fiction with (well researched, historically accurate) fiction.

Supported by the Amiel and Melburn Trust and the Lipman Milliband Trust, as well as Arts Council England.

Featuring: *Sandra Alland, Martyn Bedford, Kate Clanchy, David Constantine, Frank Cottrell Boyce, Kit de Waal, Stuart Evers, Maggie Gee, Michelle Green, Andy Hedgecock, Laura Hird, Matthew Holness, Juliet Jacques, Sara Maitland, Courttia Newland, Holly Pester, Joanna Quinn, Francesca Rhydderch, Jacob Ross, and Alexei Sayle.*

135

Iraq + 100

Stories from a Century after the Invasion

Edited by Hassan Blasim

ISBN: 9781905583669
£9.99

'I admire the achievement of this collection greatly, and I want it to be read, and celebrated, and supported. Iraq + 100 is painful, difficult, and necessary; it's often beautiful, always harrowing.' *NPR*

Iraq + 100 poses a question to ten Iraqi writers: what might your country look like in the year 2103 – a century after the disastrous American- and British-led invasion, and 87 years down the line from its current, nightmarish battle for survival? How might the effects of that one intervention reach across a century of repercussions, and shape the lives of ordinary Iraqi citizens, or influence its economy, culture, or politics? Might Iraq have finally escaped the cycle of invasion and violence triggered by 2003 and, if so, what would a new, free Iraq look like?

Covering a range of approaches – from science fiction, to allegory, to magic realism – these stories use the blank canvas of the future to explore the nation's hopes and fears in equal measure. Along the way a new aesthetic for the 'Iraqi fantastical' begins to emerge: thus we meet time-travelling angels, technophobic dictators, talking statues, macabre museum-worlds, even hovering tiger-droids, and all the time buoyed by a dark, inventive humour that, in itself, offers hope.

Featuring: *Anoud, Hassan Abdulrazzak, Ibrahim Al-Marashi, Zhraa Alhaboby, Ali Bader, Hassan Blasim, Mortada Gzar, Jalal Hasan, Diaa Jubaili, and Khalid Kaki*